Death Wishes

by the same author

Sea-Change
Wrong Man in the Mirror
Lion's Ransom
Voices in an Empty Room
Photographs Have Been Sent to Your Wife
A Mafia Kiss
Day of the Arrow
W.I.L. One to Curtis

PHILIP LORAINE

Death Wishes

St. Martin's Press
New York

Library of Congress Cataloging in Publication Data

Loraine, Philip, pseud.
  Death wishes.

  I. Title.
PR6062.067D4   1983   823'.914   83-10888
ISBN 0-312-18881-1

First published in 1983 in Great Britain by William Collins Sons & Co. Ltd.

First U.S. Edition

10 9 8 7 6 5 4 3 2 1

PART ONE

Man has his will, but woman has her way.
OLIVER WENDELL HOLMES

CHAPTER 1

By the very act of signing her name, Catherine Walden, on the hotel registration card she was dropping a pebble into a still pool of expectancy. Ripples began to spread outwards immediately: 'She's here, the daughter.'

'I didn't know there was a daughter.'

'Oh yes. By the English wife.'

'Legitimate then.'

'But certainly.'

'Why didn't she get here in time for the funeral?'

'How do I know? Am I God?' Though manifestly not God, Madame Albert, dyed auburn hair tightly curled, black eyes glittering in a mask of too much pale make-up, was the patronne of the Hôtel de la Poste and a deity in her own right.

'The mother will also come?'

'No, she's dead.'

'How do you know?'

'I asked Mademoiselle.'

'Bold!'

'On the contrary, business — a further room might have been required.'

Madame Bonnet, whose husband owned the pharmacie, was younger than Madame Albert, but not young enough for the outdated Saint Tropez look she affected: denim, sunglasses on top of streaky bleached hair, a long brown face devoid of cosmetics. 'Where did she come from?'

'New York.'

'She has brothers and sisters?'

'Not as far as one knows.'

'Then she'll be worth a fortune.'

'Yes.'

Both women sighed. 'But,' added the pharmacist's wife, brightening, 'death-duties will be vast.'

'Death-duties, pouf! A couple of those pictures will see to that. A Dégas, a Monet! Besides, he was an American, the law is different for foreign residents.'

Madame Bonnet smiled, her horse-face crinkling into the many lines imparted by too much sun. 'Certain people aren't going to like this.'

'You put it mildly.'

'She wasn't exactly expected, was she?'

'One heard no mention of her.'

The two women eyed each other with malicious rapture. Madame Bonnet said, 'You don't suppose they might . . . take steps?'

'What steps had you in mind, Françoise?'

'To . . . make things difficult for her. Perhaps even to . . . well, get her out of the way.'

'My dear, one has absolutely *no* opinion of their morals, any of them, but I hardly think they'd go as far as murder.'

'Oh, I didn't mean that.' Madame Bonnet had meant just that, but knew that her imagination was apt to run away with her. 'I was thinking more of . . . legal action.'

'Yes indeed, we may expect some interesting developments along those lines. Another glass of Porto?'

'Just a half, you're too kind. How much . . . How much do you think she knows?'

'Ah! You may well ask.'

'She gave no indication?'

'Hardly. At a first meeting.' The patronne implied that later, over other glasses of Port, further details might be revealed. This was how she kept most of her women friends, with promises of succulent morsels to come. 'The girl seems a somewhat simple and ingenuous person, you know what Americans are like.'

The pharmacist's wife nodded vaguely; she had no idea what Americans were like; neither had Madame Albert, for they never came to Montferrat, but this didn't stop her elaborating. 'One gets the impression that living so far away, never visiting him . . .'

'Never?'

'Once, to be precise.'

'Very odd!'

'You think so? Perhaps he didn't want his daughter to know . . . certain things. Would you?'

'Good God, no!'

'Exactly!' The tight little henna-ed curls bobbed up and down, all nodding together. 'So I think we may say that she's in for some nasty shocks.'

'Thank goodness I didn't go and stay with my sister in Lyon—to think of missing this! You *will* keep me informed?'

'But naturally.'

'What's she like? Attractive?'

CHAPTER 2

Catherine Walden was attractive, in a cool retiring way: slim, slight, pale hair framing the quiet oval face which was, however, capable of hardening into a determination and a sagacity which would have surprised the patronne of the Hôtel de la Poste. Her eyes were grey, perceptive. She had inherited her English mother's faultless complexion.

She was standing in the cemetery above the town, regarding the hillock of dead flowers which marked her father's grave. On top of them she had just placed a bunch of creamy yellow roses which were already beginning to wilt in the heat. She had thought it correct

to make this gesture. Even though she knew nothing
about the place it was obvious that eyes were following
her every move, yet try how she might she was unable to
muster a single sorrowful thought to lay beside the dying
flowers, a single tender memory. Well, that wasn't so
surprising.

She wondered whether his Catholicism had reasserted
itself at the last moment, whether he had died in the
bosom of the Church. Probably, they usually did; though
from all she had heard of him (she had known practically
nothing), he had never been one to hedge bets and might
not have hedged this final one.

She turned away, impatient to be elsewhere; climbed
into the small Renault, rented at Nice airport, and drove
down the hill, through Montferrat, now torpid with
siesta, and out of it in a westerly direction. But as soon as
the house came in sight all her determination suddenly
evaporated, her stomach actually turned over, and she
knew that she was incapable of performing the simple
actions she had planned: driving straight to the door,
ringing firmly, announcing herself with assurance. No,
she couldn't do it, and some old superstitious voice within
her said that it would be wrong even to try when the sense
of foreboding was so strong. Perhaps the door would open
upon a crowd of chattering people, her father's friends,
ageless, brilliant, their amused and knowing eyes turned
towards her in sudden silence. This was pure fantasy of
course, a hangover from her only visit to La Bastide ten
years before, aged thirteen.

So, instead of acting as planned she stood beside her
car and merely stared. The sun was crashing down on her
bare head, and the maquis around her pulsed in the heat
of the June afternoon, whirring and hissing with cicadas.
She looked around for solid shade; walked up the hill a
little, lizards scuttling, and leaned against a tilted slab of
rock. She was thinking about that solitary visit, how

desolately shy she had been: a plump and awkward piece of flotsam in an alien sea, tossed about on glittering waves of swift, often unintelligible, conversation, waves of laughter which had seemed to mock. So many beautiful people, in-jokes, sharp allusions, violent changes of direction, overtones and undertows. And so much frenetic movement, both physical and mental, like an endless ride on a dangerous roller-coaster — no, not so much a roller-coaster as one of those other sickening carnival machines, revolving too fast, flinging everybody to and fro, over and over, while her father sat alone at the still hub, twirling gently, enjoying the general vertigo but only sharing it vicariously.

How she had hated that visit, the puppy-fat girl of thirteen! How it had seemed to threaten and diminish her secure American life of school, friends, vacations with Aunt Elaine, her mother's sister, married to a successful doctor in Philadelphia! And yet a minute before entering the vivid enclave of La Bastide her American life had seemed all-embracing, all-important. In Philadelphia, prevailing youth-worship encouraged her to look down pityingly upon her elders; at La Bastide the elders rushed past her on eddies of talk and laughter, ignoring her, or at best, worst! flinging her a few seconds of patronizing attention.

Even her father, who should surely have drawn her close to him in parental sympathy, seemed to regard the pink and ungainly child with some chill inner amusement, forever removed. The only one who had taken any trouble to be nice to her, she remembered, was a young Englishman called Nicky, Nicholas Tate, and the only consolation to be drawn from the entire doleful experience was that he had been far and away the most beautiful of all those beautiful people.

Now, ten years later, gazing up at the long low house, prevented by the Furies of memory from approaching it,

Catherine was able to appreciate its unique quality: rock
walls easing themselves from the rocky spur on which it
stood, squat tower poised on a cliff overhanging the
maquis a hundred or so feet below, dominating the harsh
landscape as it had for centuries. The thirteen-year-old
had never noticed such things, too stricken by foreign
strangeness, just as she had never really noticed the
pictures and priceless objects which decorated the
interior.

Coming upon it all in *House and Garden* some years
later, she had at first failed to realize that this was indeed
her father's lair which she, Catherine, had once visited in
uncomprehending person: 'La Bastide de Peyrol, home of
Edward Grant Walden in the South of France.'

Fascinated, she had read:

Hidden away in a valley at the western end of the
Massif de Maures, midway between Toulon and
Saint Tropez, but too far inland to be affected by
the brash vulgarity of the coast, lies the small town of
Montferrat. Here, Edward Walden has created one
of the most beautiful small houses in Europe,
certainly one of the most secretive and unpretentious. From outside it remains what it has always
been, a semi-fortified manor farm, looking down
upon its own acres of vineyard and olive-grove, with
the rough, sweet-scented maquis beyond. Inside,
with the help of Hans Wolf, the celebrated architect
and designer, La Bastide has been enlarged and
beautified to form a completely enclosed rectangle
of heterogeneous but perfectly balanced buildings
surrounding a large courtyard-garden.

There followed many pictures of the house: the Italian
water-garden, the swimming-pool in its setting of flowers
and statues and mellow brick, glimpsed through a
cunningly contrived arcade, the circular terrace at the
base of the tower, providing all gradations of sunshine or

shade, or shelter when the Mistral swept down from the mountains: pictures of the interior, so cool, spare, elegant: pictures, finally, of the pictures.

They come as a surprise to the unprepared visitor because it is not generally known that Mr Walden is a collector. But this, one suddenly thinks, must be a Monet! And over there a pair of Blue Period Picassos dating from the days, says Edward Walden, "when he was a painter, not a publicist". And suddenly they are crowding in on one: Dégas, Guardi, Constable, Braque, a superb Giotto . . .

Her father's collection, Catherine was instructed, should not be compared with any of the *great* collections, and in fact the works were few in number. The surprise lay in their unsuspected presence and superb quality: 'perhaps the most "private", in all senses of the word, accumulation of art treasures which exists in the world today'. And she was further amazed to read that what had seemed to her, at thirteen, to be an unutterably dreary picture of an old hag, in the hall at the foot of the stairs, was in fact an unfinished study by Rembrandt.

'Hardly surprising,' concluded *House and Garden*, 'that in spite of Mr Walden's carefully cultivated reticence the locals persist in calling his hideaway "Le Château"!'

Leaning against the shady but sunwarmed rock, unable at this moment to go any closer to the 'château' which was now hers—which was certainly about to be hers—Catherine could smile at the memory of herself, standing up there, looking out over the sun-blasted valley, wondering why all those smart people kept saying, 'What a relief! one can't even *see* the Mediterranean.' (She had pined to see the Mediterranean.) Smiling, she could almost imagine that the plump little girl of thirteen was still standing on the terrace, looking down at Catherine Walden aged twenty-four.

But the figure which in fact stood on the terrace,

looking down at Catherine Walden aged twenty-four, was not that of a plump child but of a man hidden in the deep shadow cast by a tumbling bougainvillæa. He was examining her carefully through a pair of binoculars; his position had been chosen with care; the sun was beginning to slant away westwards, and no reflection on the lens would betray his presence or his intense regard.

He had no doubt that this was indeed Mademoiselle. He knew that she had arrived from New York this morning; had registered at the Hôtel de la Poste just before lunch; had eaten a hasty Croque Monsieur before going out again in the rented Renault, which he could now see parked in the uncertain shade of a group of twisted olive trees.

As far as he was concerned, the slight, defenceless-looking girl presented problems as well as possibilities. The binoculars were powerful; they revealed Catherine's smile quite clearly. Why was she smiling? What exactly did Mademoiselle, the heiress, find amusing? What indeed! the contents of the will were as yet unknown.

'How much are you going to tell her?'

'Only what I know to be true — what I *know* to be true, Julie.'

Madame Gosselin received her husband's rebuke, for rebuke it was, with a moue which, it struck him, was less attractive at fifty-two than it had been at twenty-two. A large, awkward man himself, he had spent his youth pursuing various small and pretty girls; at that age one ignored the obvious fact that they invariably grew up to become small spherical women. Madame Gosselin sighed. 'One *knows* so little.'

'Precisely.' Paul Gosselin had been on friendly terms with the dead man; had even been summoned to La Bastide for the occasional game of chess. The summonses had begun as rare winter events, for in winter the tide of pleasure-loving, sun-loving guests tended to ebb away towards the ski slopes; Edward Walden would sometimes find himself attended only by his few local friends; once or twice, God forfend! actually alone. However, with the onset of age, and illness, and the unreliable or inhospitable moods accompanying both, the invitations had come more and more frequently, even in summer. Monsieur Gosselin was a modest and exact man, as old-fashioned lawyers tend to be, and would never have claimed intimacy with his rich client, but they enjoyed the same jokes, at the expense of human folly, and the same wines, the finer Burgundies, and were well-matched at chess, both being mediocre players.

Julie Gosselin was continually irritated, as now, because although her husband knew more than anyone else about La Bastide, and the fascinating, often scandalous, things which went on up there, he resolutely refused to reveal so much as a single detail. Those matters which were not subject to professional silence were dismissed as 'mere gossip', so that either way they were not open to discussion. Madame Gosselin, like most of her friends in Montferrat, was reduced to inventing her own stories about the Walden ménage — she could hardly admit that her own husband mistrusted her! However, she never tired of trying to outwit him, and now said, 'I still find it strange that he never consulted you about his will.'

'Nothing on earth would have induced me to undertake Edward Walden's private affairs. I know my limitations.'

'Limitations, my foot! You underestimate yourself, you always have. You could have been Préfet if only you'd . . .'

Her husband sidestepped this old political plaint. 'In law the only important thing is complete understanding. His French wasn't much better than my English, there could have been disastrous mistakes.' He glanced at his watch, impatient to escape into the cool afternoon privacy of his study. Julie Gosselin smiled. 'Is she late?'

'No, no—she's not coming until five.'

'I hear she's attractive.'

'Good God, Julie, she's been in Montferrat for less than three hours, how can you have "heard" any such thing?'

'I happened to go into town for some cough syrup . . .'

'That Bonnet's an old hen. His wife's very thick with Madame Albert, I suppose the girl's staying at the Poste.'

'Correct. But why not up at the château, Paul, tell me that?'

'How would I know?'

'It's the question everyone's asking. Naturally. I intend to invite her to dinner as soon as possible.'

'That's hardly necessary, my dear.'

'Of course it's necessary. She stands to be a very rich young woman, there's no reason at all why you shouldn't handle her affairs.'

This was a typical example of the kind of baited remark, hook concealed in banality, with which she had more than once caught him napping and landed a succulent fact; but today she was out of luck; he had recognized the ploy, and all she got for her pains was a knowing chuckle and a kiss on the cheek.

Catherine was walking back to the rented Renault, deep in thought, when movement attracted her attention. A car was coming down the steep road from La Bastide, trailing a plume of dust. For no specific reason she hoped that it would turn away towards Toulon, but it did not do so; in a few minutes it would therefore drive straight past her. Why, she wondered, was her immediate reaction a desire for evasion? She considered plunging deeper into the maquis where rocks and bushes would instantly conceal her. But that was ridiculous; she had as much right to be here as anyone else: more—the land probably belonged to her. And why assume that the occupants of the car were interested in her anyway? She walked on towards the olive grove, and then realized with a leaden heart that the approaching vehicle was actually slowing down. It came to a stop some yards away, just as she reached the wavering shade of the trees.

The man who stared out at her was smooth, slick, olive-skinned, with a neat dark moustache; he looked her up and down, his regard at once appreciative and clinical. Was he, she wondered, her father's doctor? he had the look of a doctor. His black eyes flicked from her to the Renault. 'Mademoiselle is having trouble with her car?'

'No. No, thank you.' She had learned to speak French passably well during the years of aimless travel with her mother. More recently, since that disastrous visit to her father, she had even spent two vacations in France. Well away from Montferrat. 'I was just admiring the view. The house.'

'Ah, you're a foreigner, a visitor.'

'Yes.'

He nodded to himself. 'Your name would not perhaps be Walden?'

Her heart sank. She should have taken to the maquis, why didn't she pay more attention to her instincts? Equally, why should she care who knew what her name was? 'Yes, Catherine Walden.'

'How fortunate!' In spite of having recognized her, he made no effort to speak in English, but he now got out of the car, revealing himself to be of medium height, powerful and well-balanced like a lightweight boxer. He was holding something towards her. An identity card, and he wasn't a doctor, he was a policeman: Jacques Mattei, Detective-Inspector. She smiled, because in her experience policemen always expected to be disliked and were grateful for crumbs of friendliness. Inspector Mattei (was that a Corsican name? she had an idea it was) didn't look as though he'd be grateful for anything short of arrest. She said, 'How did you guess? My name?'

'You are not French. Your car was rented in Nice, I know the firm. They told me up at the château that you'd arrived in Montferrat today. From New York, I believe.'

'How would they know that?'

He smiled, a chill affair, and passed a hand over his sleek head. 'In these country places everybody knows everything.'

'And who are "they"?' For an instant she had again envisaged the house full of her father's intimidating guests, exactly as she had seen then ten years before.

'The manservant, the housekeeper.'

Catherine remembered the manservant well: an Englishman, elderly, sardonic, seeming to be on more intimate terms with her father than any of his friends and therefore an unnerving presence. The housekeeper had been a background person, seldom seen, a handsome silent young woman. But how on earth could either of them have known that she had arrived in Montferrat?

Inspector Mattei said, 'I'm glad that we chanced to meet, Mademoiselle.'

Catherine couldn't imagine why. What had he been doing at La Bastide anyway? 'Is everything all right up there?'

'Would you expect otherwise?' His tone irritated her.

'No. I just wondered what you were doing.'

The irritation and the direct approach both seemed to interest him mildly. 'You have no reason to doubt the circumstances of your father's death?'

'Good heavens, no. He wasn't a young man, he'd been ill for some time.'

'Sixty-seven is no great age.'

'It sounds as though *you* have reasons for doubt, Inspector.'

He shrugged, seeming to imply that he had a hundred reasons; then changed course abruptly. 'Of course you were not exactly close to him.'

'I saw him once in the last seventeen years.'

'So I understand.' Evidently he had said, or discovered, whatever it was that he wanted, for he now made a routine performance of glancing at his watch and finding that it was later than he'd thought. 'We shall be meeting again, Mademoiselle.'

Why would they be meeting again? He seemed quite sure of the fact. She guessed that he was waiting for her to *ask* why, and for that very reason did not do so. He accepted this with another smile and another shrug; then turned away. 'Au revoir, Mademoiselle Walden. A pleasure.'

'Au revoir, Inspector.'

He got into his car, turned it with panache, and accelerated away in the direction of Toulon.

For a time Catherine stood under the sighing silvery trees, wondering what had lain behind the seemingly pointless conversation, if anything. It had always seemed to her that petty officials created mysteries as a matter of habit: something to do with vanity. Eventually she dismissed the matter from her mind, climbed into the Renault, and drove slowly towards Monferrat: more slowly than intended, as things transpired, for she found herself trapped in the dusty wake of a local bus. The country road was narrow, and there was no hope of passing unless this lumbering conveyance were to stop. It did indeed stop, but in the centre of a drowsy hamlet where houses lined the street so closely that even a small girl bearing a loaf longer than herself could barely squeeze by.

As the bus trundled forward again, a young man shot out of the village shop clutching a paper bag, yelling at the driver to wait for him; but he was either ignored or unheard and, in his rage, took an orange from the bag and hurled it at the vehicle's broad backside. The rage,

no less than the very human and unavailing recourse to
action, made Catherine laugh. Seeing this, seeing that
she was a young and pretty girl, and doubtless well aware
of the fact that he himself was an unusually good-looking
young man, he turned to her, a pleading thumb extended
towards Montferrat.

In the United States, Catherine would never have
dreamed of giving a lift to anybody, least of all to a
handsome young man. Her motives for doing so here and
now were therefore open to question. It was possible to
say that, trapped as she was behind the bus and within a
few feet of him, she had no option. But was this the truth?
Even at the time, let alone in retrospect, she knew that it
wasn't. The truth was that as soon as she set eyes on him
there had been a slight but definite contraction in the
heart, or the gut, or wherever it is that sexual attraction
first stirs. And as soon as he got into the little car beside
her the degree of sensuality increased perceptibly; she
realized that he exuded the kind of physical presence
which hitherto she had associated only with animals: such
glossy black hair, such vividly clear and sunburned skin,
making the strong teeth seem almost dangerous, such
capable brown hands cradling the bag of oranges! He was
so perfectly the average Anglo-Saxon female's conception
of the Mediterranean male (so rarely justified!) that the
situation possessed its own kind of absurdity.

'Mademoiselle is most kind. That driver hates me.' He
spoke in rough local French, but switched languages
fluently, surprisingly, at the sound of her answer: 'Ah,
you're English.'

'More American. Part English.'

'Few tourists come this way. I like very much to speak
English.'

His assessment of her as a tourist struck her as
fortunate. In this small enclosed community she had no
wish to be recognized by all and sundry for what she really

was; she knew enough about European, as opposed to American, social divisions to realize that once she had revealed herself as Catherine Walden, heiress to 'Le Château', his free and easy attitude to her might well change. She was additionally pleased when he said, 'My name is Jean-Michel.' No surname.

'Catherine.'

'Catherine. I like that.' It sounded, she thought, more likeable with a French accent.

He explained that it was his day off; he was going to visit his aunt. 'You stay in Montferrat?'

'For a few days.'

'You must see the Abbaye de Lapalisse, it is beautiful. And you should climb Mont Bouc—nobody knows why it's called that, "bouc" is a he-goat.' He pointed to a rocky escarpment above the town. 'The view is very wide—the islands of Porquerolles on a good day.'

Feeling the heat of his tough muscular body beside her, she asked him what he did. 'I am agriculteur.' No, not a farmer, nothing as grand as that, but he was learning, he had hopes. He was studying viticulture, one day he would like to own a vineyard. An absurd picture flashed unbidden through her mind: herself as châtelaine of La Bastide, and this young man in charge of the vines which sloped away from the house in three directions. Ridiculous! She bit her lip and concentrated on driving. Whatever foolishness had urged her to give him a lift must not be allowed to run wild in such Lady-Chatterly-like fantasies. She knew nothing about him and, if she gave herself time for thought as opposed to gut reaction, was not unduly inclined to trust him: too good-looking, self-assured, conscious of his own charm.

As they approached Montferrat he said, 'If you would be so kind, my aunt lives down there.' He indicated a group of houses, a baker's shop, a café on the road. She pulled to a standstill, but he didn't immediately move; he was staring at his bag of oranges. Aware of her scrutiny he turned and smiled, but hesitantly now, no longer self-assured. 'Perhaps you . . . Would you allow me to buy you a drink?' And, with a grimace: 'In these parts we don't accept favours easily, it makes us unsure, we like to repay.' He gestured towards the café.

She intended to refuse; in fact words of refusal instantly formed themselves in her mind. But there was something in his look . . . Yes, he was expecting her to refuse. Impatient with all that was over-analytical, over-suspicious in her character — thoroughly 'New York' when she came to think of it! — she said, 'Thank you. I'm thirsty.'

He at once brightened, like a child; escorted her to the side of the café, where there were straggly fruit-trees, chickens pecking aimlessly at a scuffed yard, three elderly men practising Boule; sat her down at a chipped metal table. When he asked whether she wanted alcoholic or non-alcoholic refreshment she took another step away from that prim and untrusting girl, settling for alcohol but not too strong: her five o'clock appointment with the lawyer was important, she would need a clear head.

When he returned with their glasses she stared a little doubtfully at the cloudy pink concoction he was offering. He laughed. 'We call it "Tomate", but it has nothing to do with tomatoes, it is pastis with Grenadine, you'll like it.'

Thus instructed, she found that she did indeed like it, and found that she liked him too. Behind the country roughness, or rather walking hand in hand with it, there was an old-fashioned courtesy which touched her. Even Aunt Elaine would have approved; she was always complaining about lack of manners and consideration in the young.

They sat in the half-shade with their pastis, the bag of oranges on the table between them. She noticed now that his clothes were good, but why not? on his day off, visiting his aunt. He explained the game of Boule to her with enthusiasm, and then, ignoring her protestations, asked the old men if they might join in. 'It's okay, they aren't playing seriously, and they like to show off in front of a pretty girl.'

So it was that here, under the uncared-for peach and almond trees, chickens pecking about her feet, the brown faces of these countrymen smiling at her efforts with the heavy bowls, she suddenly felt at home and happy; the painful memory of her father's sophisticated world withdrew, seeming unimportant. She won, or was allowed to win, a game. The old men applauded. It was with real regret that she remembered her appointment and said that she must go.

Walking back to the car he was silent; the doubtful, forlorn look had reappeared. 'What are you thinking?'

He shrugged. 'I was thinking that I would like to take you out — to the Abbey of Lapalisse, or even to dinner, but . . . I have no car, not much money . . .'

'I have this car, and as for money . . .'

'No!' He was sharp. 'That is not how we think here, the man pays. But if you would care to go somewhere cheap, cheap but very good, very typical?'

It crossed her mind that he had a faculty for putting one in a position which made refusal all but impossible; and then again castigated herself for being too analytical. 'I'd like it very much.'

Again, childlike, his face cleared. 'Perhaps tomorrow? Tomorrow evening I am free of my work.'

They made it tomorrow; they would meet at seven o'clock, here at this same shabby café. When he had closed the door of the car on her he said, 'I like very much how you are — with me, with the old men. Natural. The girls here are always so . . . *affectées*, how do you say it?'

'Affected, priggish.' It was almost as if he had read her

thoughts about herself.

'Yes, that's right.'

She said, 'Until tomorrow.'

'Until tomorrow, Catherine.'

She saw in the rear-mirror that he stood staring after the car, before turning into the alleyway leading to his aunt's house. Her mood of euphoria was evaporating, she hoped she hadn't been foolish.

The young man only walked a few paces down the alley. He leaned against a wall and ate one of the oranges out of the bag, throwing the rest to a pig which was gazing at him with wrinkling snout from the other side of a fence. Then he walked back to the road. He didn't go to his aunt's house for the simple reason that he had no aunt living anywhere nearer than Lille, some five hundred miles away.

CHAPTER 3

The lawyer fended off his wife's too obviously inquisitive attentions — 'You must be tired. A glass of wine? At least a little cup of coffee?' — and steered the girl into the safe harbour of his study from which Madame Gosselin was excluded by ancient treaty.

He was almost exactly as Catherine had visualized him from that single transatlantic telephone conversation: big, benign, with an open and guileless face unusual in his profession; but there was something sharper lurking behind the greenish eyes, which was perhaps why he seldom risked more than an oblique and glancing look. A ring of hair, sandy grey, surrounded a bald, sunburned head.

'Thank you for calling me. Nobody else bothered.'

He waved a large hand. 'I'm sure that the English lawyers intended . . .'

'The fact is they did nothing.' She was incisive. He suspected that like a lot of women she made up her mind about things quickly, and that thereafter it would not be easy for her, or anyone else, to change it.

'You came here directly from New York?'

'Yes. I'm sorry I couldn't make it in time for the funeral. All the flights to Nice were booked.'

Privately Monsieur Gosselin considerd her absence fortunate. It had been a charged and awkward occasion attended by far too many busybodies who had not even known the dead man.

Catherine leaned forward. 'I need help, Monsieur, I'm completely out of my depth.'

He nodded, believing her all too completely.

'I knew my father was ill, but somehow I wasn't expecting him to die, not for years and years. And I'd never really thought about the money. That may sound weird to you, but . . . He wasn't part of my life, I guess it's as simple as that.'

Paul Gosselin nodded again, gazing at the pattern of the carpet, keeping his thoughts to himself. Catherine threw the ball squarely into his hands by adding. 'I'd like you to . . . act for me, if that's the right expression.'

The green eyes glanced at her sharply; then slid away. 'Naturally I'd be honoured, but I must tell you in all honesty that I think the English lawyers are in a better position to represent . . .'

'I don't *trust* the English lawyers. I haven't heard a word from them. Nothing.'

'Very strange. David Rudd always struck me as being most correct, most efficient.' He heaved himself upright in his chair. 'Very well, Mademoiselle, of course I'll help you to the best of my ability. That being so, we need to know certain things about each other. I must tell you that

I had no idea of your existence until your father spoke of you a couple of months before his death.'

She smiled. 'That doesn't surprise me. Did he mention my mother?'

'Never.'

'They'd had nothing to do with each other for years. I was only four when they separated, so of course I stayed with her.'

Paul Gosselin went to his desk and sat down behind it. 'Forgive me if I make notes. My memory isn't as good as it used to be. You were four years old when they separated. That would have been . . .'

'Twenty years ago, I'm twenty-four now. I only saw him once after that, when I stayed at La Bastide for a couple of weeks.'

'He told me.'

'Not a success.'

'He had no way with children, no time for them. He was a very self-centred man, you know, he frankly admitted it.'

'You knew him well.'

'Not well.'

'A hundred times better than I did.'

'What you must understand, Mademoiselle, is that I wasn't his lawyer in the full sense. I dealt only with his local affairs — the vineyard, the olives, sale or purchase of land, farm rents, that kind of thing. All the important matters were handled by Mayer, Rudd and Wilson in London.'

'Including his will, I suppose.'

'Yes.'

She glanced away and said abruptly, 'My brother died before I was born. I'm sure it shattered them both. Anyway, it was probably another reason why he ignored me. He wanted a son, sons — I suppose all men do.'

Monsieur Gosselin kept his eyes on his notes. Eventually

he said, 'I'm surprised he didn't divorce your mother and marry again.'

'They were both Catholics.'

'Yes, but . . .' He gestured. Catholic divorces were not difficult to obtain. 'He wasn't devout.'

'Neither was Mother. I think it suited them both to be married but separated. It suited her all right, she had a whole string of lovers. That was before . . . You know she died an alcoholic?'

'I knew she was an alcoholic, David Rudd told me. I wasn't sure if she was dead.'

'Two years ago.' She shook her head and sighed. 'No use pretending it wasn't a good thing. It ruined her life, it ruined her looks — well, I suppose her life *was* her looks, she was a great beauty, staggering! Poor darling, I used to get so angry with her, it all seemed so pointless! She'd sit in front of her mirror saying, "Look at me! I'm revolting," and I'd say, "You're not, you could still be lovely if only you'd stop," and she'd say, "I'm revolting, I'm *old*," and then she'd slurp some more gin, and pretty soon she *was* revolting.' There was passion in this, pity and perhaps disgust. She put both hands over her face for a moment; then lowered them and shook back her hair.

The lawyer gave her time to regain her composure. 'When did you go to America?'

'As soon as I began to get in the way.' The bitterness was as intense as the passion. More calmly, she added, 'We went there together several times. She finally dumped me on Aunt Elaine when I was ten. I don't think she meant it to be final, she just didn't want me around, she'd met the love-of-her-life. She had a new love-of-her-life every few months.'

Monsieur Gosselin shrugged and gesticulated in Gallic acceptance of this state of affairs.

'So I was left with her sister in Philadelphia, and one thing led to another, as they say, and there I stayed. Now

I expect I seem more American than English. Well, I am.'

'You work in New York?'

'Yes. I'm Personal Assistant to Rod McGregor, he's one of the advertising kings. I'm not sure how I got there, I'm not very practical.'

'I find you astonishingly practical, Mademoiselle.'

'I'm hopeless, I've even forgotten what I was trying to say. Oh yes, about the will. My mother and my brother both being dead, I suppose that makes me the only . . . whatever you call it?'

'Beneficiary. It would appear so, yes.' He was examining the tip of his pen with abnormal concentration. Catherine said, 'Well, possibly not the *only* one. He must have left something to his mistress for a start—she put up with him for a long time, didn't she?'

'I, er . . . wasn't sure if you knew about her.'

'I met her when I visited that time, she seemed nice. Isn't she Russian?'

The lawyer, now given his brief and acting on it, replied, 'Natalia Beaumont is half-Russian, on her mother's side.'

'She had an awful little boy.'

Monsieur Gosselin smiled. 'Was he awful even then? I'd forgotten.'

'He knew I was terrified of heights, so he used to dance about on that parapet—at the edge of the terrace, over the cliff. Just to scare me.'

'Yes, I can see him doing it. He's in the army now.'

'What happened to her husband?'

'She's been a widow for many years.'

'They stayed together, she and my father?'

'Yes. She was with him when he died—they were devoted.'

'I'm glad. Sometimes . . . I know I was only a kid, and an ignorant one . . .' She shuddered. 'Thirteen! That's a terrible age for girls.'

'Yes, I have two daughters of my own.'

'Then you know. What I'm trying to say is, even then I felt he was a very lonely person. Was he?'

'In the way of all rich people, yes.'

'The bigger the crowd he gathered around himself, the more lonely he seemed — to me anyway.'

'You were a perspicacious thirteen-year-old.'

She grimaced. 'I had some pretty good training, with those two for parents! You think rich people are always lonely?'

'I think they find it difficult to make friends — they're too suspicious. Hardly surprising!'

'My mother wasn't suspicious enough, she got taken left, right and centre by . . . oh, half a dozen men.'

Monsieur Gosselin was thinking that she had truly undergone a hazardous youth; yet she didn't ask for pity or sympathy as his own two daughters (both married now, thank God!) would have done, clamorously. She had survived an exacting test and had emerged very much her own person, refusing to fall back on the old feminine standbys. He found this admirable, and for that very reason proceeded with even greater caution: 'Yes, I'm sure he would have remembered Natalia Beaumont in his will, but as I say, the London lawyers dealt with all such personal matters. David Rudd came out here many times to talk business. I imagine your father made . . . various alterations to the bequests.'

Something in his tone, not entirely unintended, made her glance up at him sharply. 'You don't . . . You're not implying that he would have cut my mother out because of the way she behaved? Cut me out because of her?'

'No. He lived in France, and French law is very strict in this respect. A man has to produce overwhelming evidence against his wife or children in order to exclude them from his will. I think we can say with certainty that though he may have changed certain details — taking care

of Madame Beaumont, for instance, as you surmise — you
would remain . . . Yes, the major beneficiary.'

She nodded, apparently satisfied, and looked out of the
window. Beyond the rough red rooftops of Montferrat the
stony hills were turning pink, and the pines which swept
over them a strangely luminous black, as the sun softened
towards its setting. Bells in the three church towers began
to jangle: the Angelus. It was a time of day which
Monsieur Gosselin particularly liked; so, evidently, did
she, for her expression was peaceful. He could believe
that her mother might indeed have been a great beauty,
she was a beautiful girl herself. At length she said, 'So
when's the London lawyer . . . ? What's his name?'

'Rudd. David Rudd.'

'When's he going to appear?'

'He had planned to arrive today, but he has family
problems, poor man. His wife is very ill — she's just gone
into hospital, they operate tomorrow. He'll come
immediately afterwards. He's a charming man, you'll like
him.'

'It doesn't matter whether I do or not.' Her eyes
returned from the sunset hill and held his. 'I'll have you to
advise me.'

'I'll do my best.' The words mocked him. His best! And
here he was, allowing this sensible and straightforward
girl, who had put her trust in him, and whose entire
future depended on the matter, to remain ignorant of a
host of things which Julie and her friends discussed with
innacurate relish over coffee and little sweet cakes. But he
had said, 'I shall tell her only what I *know* to be the
truth,' and it would be unprofessional to act in any other
way: incorrect as well as dishonourable. Yet, he asked
himself, was silence really less incorrect or dishonourable?
He evaded the problem with a clumsy change of subject:
'I believe you're staying at the hotel — surely you'd be
more comfortable at La Bastide?'

'Oh no!' She was clearly horrified. 'I mean . . . Thank you, but I'd hate it. That creepy manservant!'

'Abbott isn't so bad. Like all his class he puts on airs, pretends he knows more than he does.'

'I prefer the hotel.' She smiled wryly. 'I tried to go up to the house this afternoon, but . . . my nerve failed me.' The bleak admission told him more about her childhood visit to the place, and her relationship with her parents, than anything she had hitherto said.

'You must allow me to take you there. Tomorrow.' He consulted a diary. 'Tomorrow morning. Would eleven o'clock suit you?'

'Thank you. Thank you very much.'

She only remembered the policeman as she was leaving. Monsieur Gosselin smiled. 'Ah yes, Inspector Mattei—Toulon. His manner is not calculated to be appealing, but he knows what he's doing.'

'And what *is* he doing—at La Bastide?'

'The place is full of treasures. Neither Abbott nor the housekeeper feel they can be responsible—of course they're right. The Inspector keeps two men on duty with a guard-dog.'

'Then why on earth didn't he tell me?'

'He's a Corsican, information has to be extracted, secrecy is his second nature.'

So she had been right about the Inspector's origins.

'Your father refused to have guards while he was alive, though it might have been advisable. "Terrifying my guests," he used to say, "spying on us all no doubt, and selling stories to the Press." '

She nodded, clear grey eyes searching his face. 'You must tell me what I should do, I don't belong to his kind of world. Ought I to see Madame . . . the mistress?'

'Beaumont.'

'I mean, what's correct? She's probably upset, she must have loved him.'

'Yes. Would you like me to tell her you're here? She lives not far away.'

'Please. I could visit her, if she wants to see me.'

Of course, as he well knew, Natalia Beaumont would long ago have been informed of her arrival, possibly by his own wife who could hardly be expected to resist the dissemination of such sensational news, particularly as she disliked Madame Beaumont, though she pretended the reverse.

This thought re-aroused all his mocking doubts. He was assailed by a haunting mental picture of Catherine Walden as a blind person tapping her way along the very edge of a wicked chasm, unaware of the danger yet perhaps sensing that it was there. And suddenly his cautious honesty, in this day and age when most people didn't even know the meaning of the word! struck him as ridiculous. Haltingly, unaccustomed to the vocabulary of mere guesswork, he said, 'Mademoiselle, I must ask you . . . I must warn you to keep yourself to yourself . . .'

She looked up at him, perturbed. He was getting it wrong already. 'I'm trying to say that your father's death is, naturally, a matter of consuming interest here. He was a very rich man, many famous people stayed at his house, there were all kinds of stories, a certain amount of . . . indiscretion, uninhibited parties, food for scandal. You understand me, of course.'

'Yes, I think so.'

'Don't listen to anyone, and certainly don't believe what you may hear.'

The eyes were wide now; she was frowning. Monsieur Gosselin felt sweat trickling on his back, but he persevered. 'I'm not trying to alarm you — please don't be alarmed. It's merely that you know so little, and people are . . . stupid, often cruel. They know nothing, so why should you be concerned with lies and inventions? when in a few days' time everything will be made clear.'

'You mean when Mr Rudd arrives from London.'

'Yes, and thereafter. It's very simple, Mademoiselle; don't believe anything.'

The cool regard brought him to a standstill. He had probably made a fool of himself, overstating the case and the dangers, but it was a relief to have spoken.

'Thank you,' she said. 'I think I understand, more or less.'

She dined alone at the hotel, a corner table, her back to the wall. Madame Albert made quite sure that any of the other diners who were interesed, 98% of them, knew who she was. The curious glances, swiftly averted if Catherine met them, the murmured conversations, heads drawing closer together, were a verification of Monsieur Gosselin's warnings.

His solicitude had touched her; pleased her too, because it meant that she had succeeded in convincing him of her need for advice and protection. She was not altogether as ingenuous as he had supposed; at various times, usually after four or five Martinis, her mother had fired off numerous suggestive remarks, so that even when Catherine had visited La Bastide as a child she was able to recognize, if incompletely, the various sexual games and permutations which seemed to occupy so much of everybody's time. She often thanked God for the freedom which allowed her own generation to make something less laborious out of these transactions. 'But you miss so much *fun!*' her mother had cried, mourning the forbidden fruit which now fell, rotten and unheeded, from the tree.

Dining alone was not one of her favourite occupations, but at least the French accepted solitary people, even women, with civilized tact: unlike the Americans and the British. In any case she wasn't unused to being alone, an only child with two absentee parents, and she had a great deal to think about.

Again thanks to her mother's tipsy reminiscences, as well as to other sources of information, she knew that her father had indulged in an assortment of love-affairs. If Madame Natalia Beaumont had been with him at the end, it simply meant that after all those years, more than twenty, they had remained good friends. Madame Beaumont had been her mother's exact contemporary, they had attended some finishing-school together. (Did finishing-schools still exist in Europe? They sounded incredibly dated.) Laura Walden had said more than once, 'Thank God the old fool's got Natalia to look after him!' Not a trace of jealousy as far as Catherine could discern, but in fact her mother didn't have much to be jealous about, passing devotedly from one love-of-her-life to the next. And then, quite suddenly, for no rational reason, that wilful self-destruction had begun; within a few months the beautiful butterfly had turned into a raddled sot swilling gin in a darkened room; within a few years the destruction was complete.

In retrospect, Catherine found that she was not unduly troubled by Monsieur Gosselin's warnings. Of course the future probably held surprises, even shocks, but if life had taught her anything, it had taught her how to cope with shocks and surprises. She was impatient for Mr Rudd to appear from London and settle matters once and for all, and it was doubly reassuring to know that French law was on her side. That being so, it hardly mattered how many skeletons might be lurking in her father's cupboard. She went up to bed well satisfied with this, the first day of her return to Montferrat.

It was to end on a lighter note. As she opened her window, overlooking the garden of the hotel, not the noisy Place de la République with its buses and its cafés, a dark figure detached itself from darkness below her. She heard, 'Tst-tst!' and caught the glimmer of very white teeth in a brown face. Hardly raising his voice he said,

'Tomorrow at seven, the same café. Don't forget!'
  She laughed softly. 'Of course I won't forget.'
  'Bonne nuit, Catherine. Pleasant dreams.'
  'Bonne nuit, Jean-Michel. Idiot!'
  He too laughed; raised a hand; rejoined the shadows. A
meaningless piece of Southern gallantry no doubt, but it
sent her to bed feeling warmed, amused, less alone.

CHAPTER 4

Perhaps her decision of the day before, not to proceed up
the hill and enter La Bastide, had been dictated by
something more profound than a handful of unhappy
memories. Even with Monsieur Gosselin at her side the
visit was to prove ominous.
  It started harmlessly enough, in that the manservant,
Abbott, when he opened the door, was revealed as being
much older, much milder, than she had remembered. He
was thin, with a narrow melancholy face, grey hair cut
very short, an ambassadorial manner, a matching voice
which had long since lost its London zest; but his eyes, of
a pale washed-out blue, were preternaturally sharp,
suggesting that another person altogether was trapped
behind the solemn façade, or was using it as a front for
something deceitful.
  'Nice to see you again, Miss. Ah, you've fined down, as
they say, since your last visit. If I may make so bold, all
those young fellows would be paying you a lot more
attention now.' Thus, instantly, he told her that he well
remembered her former awkwardness and the lack of
popularity engendered by it. He hadn't changed much
after all.
  Catherine ignored him, allowing her eyes to stray
towards the Rembrandt at the foot of the stairs. Of

course! It was unmistakable—what a lot one learned in the years between thirteen and twenty-four!—a preliminary study, perhaps, for the portraits of his mother, one of which she had seen at some stately home in England.

Double doors were open to what was known as the salon. The early Dégas leapt forward to surprise her, vivid, full of life and high spirits. Shuttered sunlight slanted across the beautiful room, creating a golden haze of polished wood, inlay, ormulu. A Rodin figure hesitated near the door. Beyond it a magnificent buhl clock struck the half-hour. The pendant at the bottom of one of the chandeliers twirled slowly through the spectrum . . . and from the swimming-pool outside came the sound of raised voices and laughter.

Instantly, Catherine stepped back ten years. Her heart went down like a stone into icy depths. She knew that they were indeed all there, as they had been in her nightmare fantasy, unchanged and disturbing. Abbott's faded eyes were watching her intently; or so she imagined.

Monsieur Gosselin said sharply, 'What's that? Who's out there?'

Leading them forward into the arcaded walk, Abbott replied, 'Mr Tate arrived for the funeral, sir, as I believe you know. Madame Beaumont came over to collect some of her things.' And there they were, he on his back in the clear green water, she at the brink, laughing down at him. Abbott said, 'I informed them that you and Miss Walden were coming, sir.'

'Why then didn't you inform me that they were here?'

Abbott chose not to answer this question, but the pale eyes seemed to say that he had considered it more entertaining to arrange the encounter like this; and at the same moment Catherine received her first intimation that she had not in the least understood Monsieur Gosselin's warnings. She moved forward beside him, her mind slipping and floundering.

Natalia Beaumont turned with a smile of welcome. She had aged too, but possessed the kind of Russian bones which are made for aging; she still looked beautiful, black hair swept back to a chignon, a turquoise silk dress of the utmost simplicity (and of the utmost audacity, considering her years) swung with her turn and settled into impeccable folds. Catherine had forgotten, or had possibly never realized at thirteen, that she was so like the accepted image of a ballerina. 'Ah,' she said in English, 'Abbott has said that you were expected. How like your mother you have become! Monsieur Gosselin.'

Nicholas Tate, Catherine's single cavalier of ten years before, had climbed out of the pool. She saw that he was no longer a golden boy—he must now be in his middle thirties—and he was not as tall as she had imagined. The faun's face, in which laughter and mockery always seemed to be mixed, beguilingly, had not aged as well as the slim body; there were lines of tension or anxiety. 'Do you remember me? Nicky Tate.'

'Yes, of course.' She heard her own voice and was surprised by its even tone. 'And Madame Beaumont. I remember it all as if it was yesterday.'

'Thank God it isn't!' He flung a towel around his shoulders; the gentle brown eyes met hers for a moment, then glanced away.

Natalia Beaumont was laughing at Monsieur Gosselin's expression. 'Paul, Paul, don't look so cross!'

'I didn't know you were here, either of you.'

'Well, here we are, you'll have to make the best of us. I have a whole suite full of things which must be packed up and taken away.'

Catherine was thinking that this house, this 'château', had been more their home than it had ever been hers. And she was, yes, irritated to realize that Nicholas Tate was in residence, perfectly at ease, while she, who would have been perfectly ill-at-ease, crouched down there at the Hôtel de la Poste. She wanted some kind of clarification, and said to him, 'I didn't know you were staying here.'

'Yes. My old room's never been changed.'

Evidently Madame Beaumont could recognize a potentially awkward situation from a great distance. She laughed affectionately. 'Edward used to say, "As long as it's there, Nicky will keep coming back," and he was right.'

'God knows why he *wanted* me to come back!'

'He was fond of you and he was always loyal to his friends.'

His old room had never been changed—what exactly did that mean? Catherine, the young visitor, had supposed that he was just another summer guest, like everyone else. She looked at him curiously, but he had turned away and was drying his fair hair.

Abbott, having as it were betrayed Monsieur Gosselin, now deferred to him with paper-thin deference: 'Will you be staying to luncheon, Monsieur?'

'No, no—I have to . . .' He looked at Catherine. 'Unless of course you . . . ?'

The idea of being stranded at La Bastide with these two ambiguous people who were part of a life which was not her life, stranded without the lawyer, her ally, struck Catherine with horror. She lied: 'I've arranged . . . I'm having lunch with a friend.'

'Ah!' The other woman's eyes were level. 'You didn't come to Monferrat alone.'

'Yes, I came alone. This is . . . a young man I met yesterday.'

Madame was obviously thinking, 'Fast worker!' but she said, 'Then, alas, it will be only two for lunch, thank you, Abbott. Nothing much for me—as much as you would give a mouse.'

Abbott smiled; and in a flash of intuition Catherine

was sure that this was because La Bastide sheltered many mice and the only food Abbott would consider giving them for lunch was rat poison. The washed-out eyes slipped across her face, noted her sharing of his little joke, if that's what it was, and then turned downwards. 'Very good, Madame.'

There was now an hiatus. The unspoken purpose of Catherine's visit had been to examine the house and its contents: her possessions, or mostly hers. This would have been possible alone with Monsieur Gosselin, her legal adviser; it certainly wasn't possible now that the whole thing had turned into an unwanted social occasion.

However, Natalia Beaumont was not one to let any hiatus get the better of her; she called after the retreating manservant, 'Abbott? Some champagne, please.' He gave a little bow of acknowledgement. She turned to Catherine, 'Your father always liked champagne between eleven and twelve—the only time of day for it, he used to say. Come!' She slipped an arm through the girl's arm and looked at Monsieur Gosselin. 'We should talk together. Let's leave these men to their sulking.'

The lawyer shrugged; then smiled. 'Abbott irritated me.'

'Abbott's been irritating us all for years. He's only here because Edward liked him. Now Edward has gone, Abbott must go too. He knows it. I can't think what he's waiting for.'

Nicholas Tate looked over his shoulder at her. 'Don't be disingenuous, Natalia. He's waiting for the reading of the will—like everyone else.'

She gave him a hard look and drew Catherine away down an alley of roses, yellow and white, in brief Mediterranean full bloom. She said, 'Paul's right—that was naughty of Abbott, it gave you a shock to see us.'

'I was hoping it didn't show.'

'You're much too young to be able to hide such things.

Tell me, how's your poor mother?'

Catherine came to a stop, staring. 'Didn't you know? She died, two years ago.'

Madame Beaumont returned the stare for a moment; then glanced away. 'How typical of Edward not to mention it!'

'Did he never talk about her?'

'Never by his own wish. Only if some old mutual acquaintance forced him to it — and *they*'ve grown fewer over the years. Did she talk about him?'

'Once or twice, when she'd had a few drinks.'

'In a kindly way?'

'No, not really.'

The older woman shook her head. 'They were once so much in love.' And, smiling: 'I was a bridesmaid. We all had dark hair and we wore the palest, palest yellow-green. With your mother being so fair, in white . . . Quite *a coup de théatre!* Or should one call it a *coup d'église?* As for Edward . . . Well, of course I fell in love with him then and there, we all did. And such a brilliant diplomatic career!' She sighed. 'A pity about all that!'

'Why did he give it up? Mother would never explain.'

'Oh, he was much too naughty for the Corps Diplomatique, much too clever, much too rich. Nicky Tate looks . . . frantic, don't you think? Or perhaps you can't remember him the way he used to be.'

Was this an uncharacteristically clumsy change of subject, or did the two subjects, the Diplomatic Service and Nicholas Tate, interlock in some way? 'Of course I remember him, he was so sweet to me. And yes, he is . . . he has changed.'

'Pursued. Or driven. It's not money, I'm told he's doing very well.' And in answer to Catherine's questioning silence: 'Antique furniture. London, New York, Los Angeles. Edward gave us both the money to get started — I'm "Éclat" all down this coast, you can hardly miss me. Monte Carlo, Nice, Cannes, Marseille, six others in between. Beauty parlours—the best.' She gave the girl a look of professional assessment. 'You don't need us, you're very nice as you are.'

These revelations of her father's philanthropic activities surprised Catherine; he had seemed much too self-centred to even consider helping his friends in their business ventures. Suspecting this, perhaps, the other woman said, 'It's a pity you never knew him better. He was two very different people, one of them so concerned and thoughtful, the other . . . But I suppose we're all of us both Jekyll and Hyde.' She picked a white rose and moved on. Catherine, beside her, was again unable to quell a flare of jealousy; the very act of picking the rose proved so conclusively that this woman was at home here whereas she was not. Unable to stop herself, she said, 'It'll be terrible having to sell the place.' She had kept her eyes on Madame Beaumont and noted that *she* was certainly old enough to hide any shock she might be feeling: if indeed the remark had shocked her at all. 'Perhaps,' she said mildly, 'Edward's will makes . . . some kind of provision. He loved La Bastide.'

Catherine hadn't thought of this, but irritation or jealousy, or whatever it was, forced her to go on: 'I know *I* won't want to keep it.'

Natalia Beaumont was silent, twirling the rose against her cheek. 'Naturally it means little to you.' And, after another pause: 'How much has Paul Gosselin told you about the will?'

'Nothing, he doesn't know anything. It's all in the hands of the London lawyers.'

'Ah!' The soft exclamation seemed at first to imply simple agreement; and then, emerging slyly from the shadows of the garden, all kinds of other unquiet meanings began to creep up on Catherine. Supposing she was wrong in every conceivable way—had been purposely misled? Again, and more forcibly, she was struck by the suspicion that she had not understood Monsieur Gosselin's warnings at all. It was possible that he hadn't told her anything like the truth: out of misplaced sympathy, or because his loyalties lay elsewhere.

Evidently her youth had again revealed too much of her thoughts, because Madame Beaumont again slipped an arm through hers and said in a practical, unambiguous tone, 'We shall all have to wait for David Rudd, who arrives, I'm told, the day after tomorrow.' Then, changing the subject deftly: 'Now, let me be purely inquisitive, you must know by now how incurably inquisitive we all are around here, and ask you about the young man you met so swiftly and who is to steal you away from us at lunch-time.'

'Oh . . . just somebody I . . . Actually I gave him a lift. He was very charming, he wants to show me some Abbey.'

'Lapalisse.'

'Yes.'

'What's his name, I'm sure to know him.'

Impossible to admit that they had never exchanged surnames! 'Isn't it awful, I've forgotten, I should have written it down. Jean-Michel something.'

The reaction was extraordinary. Madame Natalie Beaumont, so adept at smoothing over hiatus situations and hiding shocks, jerked her arm away and stared, wide-eyed. That being done, there was no retrieving the situation, and she was too clever to try. She said, 'How strange! What's he like?'

'Very black hair, strong, good-looking, he's a kind of student farmer, learning about the care of vines. Why strange?'

The eyes, which Catherine had supposed to be brown but which, during this moment, she had perceived to be a strange shade of deep violet, were now hidden by delicate lids, immaculately false eyelashes. 'Because . . . Oh, ridiculous! I once had a friend called Jean-Michel, it was a shock to hear the name again.' This wasn't an adequate explanation, it wasn't even supposed to be one; it merely cobbled together their split conversation. And as a last stitch Madame added, 'We should go back before those two drink all the champagne.'

There was no way of telling whether the men's conversation had been as surprising as that of the two women among the roses, but certainly the convivial-seeming ceremony of drinking Edward Walden's wine together failed to draw them into any more profound affinity. Monsieur Gosselin was abstracted and clearly wanted, or needed, to be elsewhere. Nicholas Tate had receded into his own thoughts, which might well have been tortuous: he was too young for those deep lines, not unattractive, which scored the still beautiful face from nose to corners of mouth. Madame Beaumont merely relaxed, perhaps tired of trying to hold them all together. And Catherine, cheated in her purpose of visiting the house, now wanted only to get away from it; she found its atmosphere as stifling today as she had found it ten years before; also she wanted to ask the lawyer a few questions.

Monsieur Gosselin, as if realizing this and not relishing the prospect, led her back to his car by a roundabout route: down a long gallery full of valuable objects which no longer interested her, through an imposing library which she couldn't remember having seen before, across the salon, where even Dégas, Manet, Guardi, and (she remembered from *House and Garden*) a bronze head by Praxiteles, failed to divert her.

As soon as Monsieur Gosselin had climbed into his car beside her she said, 'Who *is* Nicholas Tate? Why does he have his own room there?'

'Years ago, Edward Walden employed him to catalogue the collection, a considerable undertaking — for which we shall now be grateful, at least everything is listed. It took him a very long time, naturally.'

She had a feeling that he had been preparing this answer from the moment Mr Tate had made the remark about his 'old room'; he was no fool, his eyes had told her that at their first meeting.

'Then . . . he'd be here now in connection with the will — valuation and so on?'

'Presumably. I didn't summon him, the London lawyers must have done so. And of course he wanted to attend the funeral.' Perhaps he felt that all this sounded too pat, because he added, 'In any case Natalia is right, your father was always loyal to old friends.'

'You never told me he'd set them both up in business.'

'Did he? I wasn't aware of it. I believe he could be extremely generous at times, I don't suppose they were by any means the only ones he helped.'

'Madame Beaumont implied that . . . that you knew things about the will which you're not telling me.'

He smiled, not the reaction she had expected. 'Natalia is sometimes indiscreet.'

'But do you? And if so, *why* haven't you told me?'

'Mademoiselle, I see that this encounter has disturbed you. I was afraid it might, which is the reason I was so annoyed with Abbott. I warned you against listening to local tittle-tattle, let alone believing it. You have far too much good sense to want me, your lawyer and I hope your friend, to compound the stupidity by tittle-tattling myself.'

She was silent, watching the maquis flash by, loud with ceaseless cicadas, enjoying the dry herbal scent of it. 'You mean, you don't know anything, you've only heard stories.'

'Everybody in Montferrat has heard stories, or is busy inventing them. One is that he proposed to endow La Bastide as a museum, another that he is leaving it all to Abbott who will convert it into a luxury hotel. I'm sure the proverbial Cat's Home has not escaped mention.'

Catherine was now ashamed of herself for having turned on him in such obvious doubt. He added, 'I resolved to tell you only what I *know* to be true, and I have.'

'I'm sorry.'

'There's no need. It was inevitable that you'd be disconcerted sooner or later. I tried to help you a little in advance, but it seems that I only . . .'

'No, you did help me.' She looked at him, very large in the small car, and very hot, massive hands clamped to the steering-wheel, eyes resolutely ahead. 'Why was Madame Beaumont so shocked when I told her that the boy I met yesterday was called Jean-Michel?'

He grimaced. 'Perhaps because it's the name of her own son.'

'Her son! But he was called . . . yes, Moko.'

'That was his nickname when he was little.' And, with an amused glance, 'Don't worry, Mademoiselle, it wasn't him you met yesterday, he's with his unit at Besançon. I told you he was in the army, didn't I?'

'Yes.'

'Jean-Michel is not a very unusual name.'

'Oh. Just a coincidence then?'

'Apparently.'

Catherine didn't altogether believe in coincidences. 'But why was she so shocked?'

'It would be unlike her. Perhaps you misread the reaction.'

Catherine shook her head; there'd been no misreading of that particular reaction. Noticing her expression, Monsieur Gosselin enquired, 'What did he look like, your young man?'

Once again, to the best of her ability, she described Jean-Michel. Monsieur Gosselin shrugged. 'Black-haired, sturdy, an agriculteur, there must be a hundred such, it's the local type. Natalia's son is fair.' And, with a dry smile, 'I take it you're not having lunch with him — that was an excuse.'

'Oh God! The idea of being stuck up there with those two.'

'Very wise. In the circumstances.'

'But it wasn't a complete lie, I'm having dinner with him tonight. He's going to show me the Abbey at Lapalisse.'

'Lapalisse will be en féte, it's their Saint's Day, Saint Gilles. You might find that entertaining.'

'He didn't mention it.'

'Wishing perhaps to surprise you.'

'Perhaps.' Something instinctive forbade her to accept this reasonable explanation, just as she had been unable to accept the earlier coincidence. Monsieur Gosselin was probably correct: she was allowing the entire situation to get on her nerves; on the other hand she knew better than to ignore her instincts altogether, they were sometimes remarkably astute. 'Perhaps. Time will tell.'

CHAPTER 5

Jean-Michel was waiting for her when she got to the café a little after seven. She had made up her mind that she was going out to enjoy herself and would leave all nagging suspicions and questions behind; but as soon as he said, 'How smart you look! I'm flattered,' she heard herself replying, 'I thought it was the least I could do to honour Saint Gilles.'

He struck his forehead. 'I forgot. And you knew all the time.'

'Not all the time, somebody happened to mention it today.' Was it likely that a local boy would 'forget' such

an important local occasion? Not likely but possible — for
God's sake, Catherine, give him a chance!

He said, 'There'll be quite a crowd. Perhaps you'd
rather not . . . ?'

'No, it'll be fun. Won't it?'

He grimaced and see-sawed spread fingers. 'Let's see.'

Thinking it correct, she asked him to drive. He drove
well; even if he didn't own a car he was obviously used to
them. Before they were out of Montferrat he said,
pointblank, 'What would your boy-friend in the States
think about this?'

She considered the question, and on the whole found it
rather pleasing. He was taking it for granted that she was
too attractive not to have a boy-friend in America, and at
the same time he was stating quite frankly that as far as
he was concerned there was some kind of sexual contract
involved in the expedition. Of course there was; a girl
didn't go out for the evening with a young man unless she
had already put her signature to such a contract, even if it
implied no more than a kiss on the doorstep at parting.
'My boy-friend's fed up with me just at the moment, he
was quite relieved when I said I was going away.'

This was true, except that she and Steve had actually
parted company a week before she heard of her father's
death. It was nothing new in her life; the fact was that
emotionally she demanded too much — for blatant
psychological reasons which she could recognize but was
unable to control.

Jean-Michel accepted the reply at its face value.
Obviously he was a young man who preferred his
contracts to be clear and unambiguous. It struck her that
despite surface differences they were in some indefinable
way rather alike.

Lapalisse was a 'ville perchée'. The old houses climbed
almost vertically towards the Abbey on top of the hill, the
roof of the building below making a terrace for the one

above. It was a town of steep streets and three-sided
squares, the fourth side consisting of a low wall and a
dizzying vista.

The Abbey, very ancient, solid, once fortified, was
floodlit for its great day, and the market-place in front of
the west door was full of booths and sideshows. No
raucous carnival machines here, but diversions from a
quieter age: coconut-shies, a gipsy fortune-teller, a simple
form of roulette played on a kind of clock-face, Hoopla.
Solemn infants in their Sunday best revolved sedately on a
battered little roundabout, and from time to time the
proceedings were punctuated by a dominant clang,
evidence that some young man had proved himself on the
strength-testing machine.

The smells were many-layered, wholly foreign: not
even a trace of the popcorn which in Catherine's mind
could hardly be disassociated from such an occasion, but
roasting almonds in vanilla-ed sugar, pastis, fragrant
crêpes, generous wafts of garlic. The two cafés were
packed with drinkers, most of the men's faces as ruddy as
the local red wine, most of the women's as pale as the acid
white. Amid the hubbub a small girl slept peacefully with
her head on a table.

Catherine and Jean-Michel lit flaring candles in front
of Saint Gilles who, for this occasion, occupied a dais on
the steps outside his church, seeming in his gaudy pomp
to have more in common with the merrymaking in the
market-place than with the cool and silent Abbey behind
him.

In the end, unwilling to leave the hub of activity for a
quieter restaurant down the hill, they dined under the
Saint's eye, sitting side by side on his steps: prawns from a
paper twist, magnificent cheese crêpes, too hot to hold,
washed down with a bottle of wine, followed by sugared
almonds and fingers of crystallized orange-peel. Then
Jean-Michel tried his strength and succeeded in ringing

the bell; Catherine won a woolly rabbit at Hoopla and he
a bottle of cheap champagne at the shooting gallery; they
performed the customary ritual of exchanging these
prizes with a kiss. All the time, as he steered her through
the crowd or pushed his way forwards so they could see
the fire-eater, she was aware of him touching her more
often, holding her more closely. It was pleasant to be
touched and held by him; he did it well, with warm
animal assurance; and presently, as expected, this
conventional overture led them to a grove of pine-trees
flanking the southern wall of the Abbey, where they
settled down to drink their champagne out of paper cups
borrowed from a Pepsi-Cola stand.

The dry pine-needles were soft and aromatic, the place
was removed from the noise and the glare, nor were they
the only couple who had sought privacy there. He kissed
her expertly and she responded with pleasure. They
drank more champagne, which was not very good, and
indulged in more kissing, which was admirable.

They lay back for greater comfort, and perhaps the
whole thing would have led, gently and inevitably, to an
ecstatic conclusion if at a certain moment a car, climbing
the steep hill, had not swung around a corner far below:
if the reflection from its headlights had not for an instant
shown her something disquieting about the young man's
handsome face descending with parted lips on to her own.

Later, she was unable to define exactly what it was that
she had seen and why it had affected her so strongly.
Perhaps the merest glint of amusement in the dark eyes,
at once ironical and calculating. Whatever the reason,
she suddenly felt sure that he was playing a game with
her, quite apart from the conventional sexual game in
which they were united. She turned her head away
sharply, evading his lips.

'No?'

'I . . . No, not here, not like this.' Of course that was a

convention too, slipshod, but it would have to do.

It seemed to her that he removed himself a little too quickly. Surely the normal male reaction would have been to chide and insist, forcing her to respond, and only then, finding no response, to give up with a bad or good grace? But this instant acceptance, coupled with such a sardonic look, could only mean that he had anticipated the denial, and even in some devious way planned that she should deny him. It was an unnerving inference, but she couldn't avoid it. All her suspicions came flooding back.

Lying by her side on the soft carpet of pine-needles, he said, 'I'm sorry. Perhaps we do things differently here, perhaps we are more . . . impatient?'

'It isn't that.' She turned her head, searching the attractive face, finding in it none of the things which might be expected, particularly in this part of the world: no sexual pique, no hurt pride; he was remarkably, even insultingly, impassive.

'Really,' she said, 'I . . . I like you very much.'

And he, turning his shadowed eyes upon her, replied, 'And I like you very much too, Mademoiselle Walden.'

It was not so much the fact that he knew her name, and had presumably known it all along; no, far more troubling was his choice of this particular moment to use it for the first time: mocking her, for there had been a distinct edge of malice in his voice. So much for her discordant instincts! Right again!

She sat up and shook back her hair. With a solicitude which was almost derisive, he brushed pine-needles from the back of her dress. She said, 'How long have you known who I was?'

'From the moment of meeting you—or before. Why? Does it matter?'

'No, of course not.'

He laughed softly; he knew what she was thinking:

local farmer's boy on the make picks up heiress to the Walden fortune. She was aware of herself colouring in the half-darkness.

'Alas,' he said, suddenly lapsing into French, as if English had been a ploy which could now be dispensed with, 'I'm afraid our evening is ruined.'

She peered at him; no passing car to illuminate his expression, only a gleam of light in the black eyes. 'May I offer you a drink, Mademoiselle, before we return to Montferrat?'

'No, thank you, I've had enough. Perhaps too much.'

He laughed softly. She felt that her implication, that only alcohol had led her to this grove of pines, to this impasse, deserved his mockery. And he was right, of course: the evening had been robbed of its climax, there was no retrieving it, no pleasure or purpose to be gained from returning to the preliminaries.

So they walked through the merrymaking to her rented car, and drove back to Montferrat. The woolly rabbit which she had given him sat against the windscreen observing their silences, their attempts at conversation — or rather her attempts, for Jean-Michel seemed quite content not to try.

He asked her to stop at the usual place, near the café. She did so. 'Will you stay with your aunt? Can't I drive you to . . . to wherever you live?'

'No thank you, Mademoiselle. I shall have a cognac and then walk home, it's not far.' He got out of the car and looked at the rabbit with raised brows; finally decided to take it.

Feeling inadequate and in some way in the wrong (but that was absurd!) she said, 'Thank you. I enjoyed my evening, I really did.'

'Not as much as I. No, I mean it. Next time we shall perhaps . . . get to know each other better.'

She refused to answer this mockery. He made the

rabbit bow to her. She said, 'Good night, Jean-Michel,' and drove away.

When she was out of sight he crossed the road and entered, not the café but the yard behind it where his own car, a sporty silver Mercedes, was standing. He got into it, placed the rabbit against the windshield, as before, and sat regarding it for a time, deep in thought. Then he started the engine and drove off in the opposite direction.

He realized, as soon as he saw the lighted windows, that his mother was waiting up for him. Nothing unusual about that, she often waited up, and often they laughed together over his exploits. Possibly because they were alone together in the world, there was very little parent and child insularity about their relationship; in many ways they were more like an eldest sister and a youngest brother. As always, he looked forward to seeing her, but the expectation turned sour when he opened the front door and heard voices: sourer still when he found that her visitor was none other than Madame Natalia Beaumont. The two women looked up at him over cups of tisane, analytical, unsmiling. He returned their stare evenly.

At length his mother, a handsome woman in her early forties, thickening now as all the local women did, but still retaining traces of a remarkable Mediterranean beauty, said, 'Pascal, you're playing games, what are you up to?'

'That's a fine welcome.' He went to a corner-cupboard, took out a bottle of cognac and a glass, glanced around at them. 'Won't you join me?'

His mother shook her head and Madame Beaumont said acidly, 'There are pine-needles on the back of your shirt, from which I deduce that you've been lying down.'

'You know how it is — one gets weary.'

'Pascal!' threateningly, from his mother; she knew him too well. 'Madame Beaumont spoke to Monsieur Gosselin

on the phone. They'd both already guessed it was you.
Please tell us what on earth you think you're doing?'
  'My God, she's a pretty girl, I took her out — so?'
  'So,' said Natalia Beaumont, 'you told her a pack of lies
about being a student-agriculteur, and you used my son's
name — please don't tell me that was by chance.'
  'Tante Natalie, you're being unreasonable.'
  'I am not your aunt, and my name is Natalia.' She
looked at Madame Lavallier in silent angry criticism. The
younger woman sighed and ran a hand through her hair,
black like her son's, but curly. 'Yes, yes, he's impossible.
God knows, I've tried, but . . . You know what they're
like.'
  'If allowed to be, yes.' And to the young man: 'What
have you told her?'
  'About?'
  'About Edward Walden's will — don't be obtuse!'
  'Madame Natalia,' carefully enunciated, 'it's not a
subject which interests me in the very least. What's more,
I know nothing.'
  'That,' said his mother, 'has never stopped you in the
past!'
  'And anyway,' said Pascal, downing the cognac and
refilling his glass, 'why shouldn't she be told anything she
wants to know? Why the secrecy?'
  Madame Beaumont stood up and faced him angrily. 'If
Jean-Michel were here he'd teach you a lesson you
wouldn't forget.'
  'He could always try.'
  She swung around on Madame Lavallier. 'This farce
has gone on long enough. I shall talk to Monsieur Gosselin
tomorrow — he's a nice man but sometimes he can be a
perfect fool.'
  When the door had closed upon her, Madame
Lavallier turned and looked at her son. 'Tante Natalie
indeed! you're impossible.' But she couldn't hide her

amusement, and he knew as well as everyone else in
Montferrat that there was no love lost between the two
women. 'Come on, Mother, you're dying for a cognac.'

'It's the truth.'

He turned away to pour her a glass, and felt her fingers
plucking at the back of his shirt. 'Pine-needles! You
didn't . . . do anything with her?'

'We didn't fuck if that's what you mean. Here, drink
up!'

'Pascal!'

'Oh come off it, Mother!'

'What's she like?'

He grinned; he had known that her natural curiosity
couldn't lie dormant for long. 'She's a lovely girl.'

'I bet she finds Monferrat dull, after New York.'
Madame Lavallier had romantic, often absurd ideas
about foreign parts; her greatest ambition was to travel. 'I
wonder if she came on one of those big planes.'

'All the planes from New York are big.'

She went nearer to him, frowning now, her peasant
nature fighting with other more sophisticated influences.
'Pascal, promise me you didn't . . . do anything?'

'I promise, Mother.'

'On the Cross?'

'On the Cross.'

They both drank a little cognac, eyeing each other,
very alike in their dark, earthy good-looks. 'Not, he added
wickedly, 'for want of trying!'

She tried to remain stern and was unable to do so:
'Pascal, you're *dreadful*, what can I do with you?' But
they had both dissolved into laughter.

CHAPTER 6

Catherine was having her breakfast on the hotel terrace when the telephone call came through. Madame Albert, blackcurrant eyes vivid with curiosity, summoned her personally and loitered not far away in order to catch any crumbs of information which might fall.

Nicholas Tate's voice sounded fresh and young, at variance with his looks. 'Listen — I know yesterday was a disaster. Due to that bloody Abbott, as usual, there never was such a diabolical mixer.'

'It didn't matter.'

'It did and it does. You came up to see the house, and all you got was Natalia and me and Abbott's bitching. But I tell you what —' he went on quickly before she could find any more false protestations — 'I shall be out today, and Natalia won't be here, she's got a meeting in Cannes. Why don't you come up on your own? I'll tell Abbott to behave himself and give you a nice lunch.'

No use trying to pretend in the face of such frank friendliness. She said, 'I'd like that.'

'Of course you would. What do you want to eat?'

'Not much. I'm never hungry in the middle of the day.'

'Leave it me, eh? And Catherine, I tell you what — tomorrow or some time let's go somewhere nice for dinner, somewhere really good, grand-luxe.'

'Fine.'

'We'll be in touch. What time do you want to get here?'

'Half past ten, eleven.'

'I'll organize the monster, and if you get any cheek, slap him down.'

'Sure.'

'Good girl! See you.' He replaced the receiver and

looked at Natalia Beaumont who was sitting on the other side of his breakfast table, elegant in pale peach chiffon. 'Shall I make the date with Gosselin?'

'I'll do it, finish you're melon. Eleven o'clock to be on the safe side, we don't want her to see us.'

'She'll be here at ten-thirty sharp, if I know anything about it. We must tell Abbott that we want a blow-by-blow account of everything she does.'

Eyeing his smile, Natalia Beaumont said, 'Your horns are showing.'

The manservant greeted Catherine civilly enough, no personal remarks today. He said, 'Mr Tate left a package for you, Miss.' A weighty manila envelope. 'Luncheon on the terrace at one — would that be to your liking?'

'Thank you, Abbott, perfect.'

During this brief exchange a large lazy-looking man with a black moustache, who could have been nothing but one of Inspector Mattei's underlings, appeared in the background attached by chain to an over-energetic Doberman. He gave Catherine a hard stare, no doubt memorizing her features in case she should tuck the Rembrandt under her arm and make a dash for it. Wearily, and at the same time giving the dog a wide berth, Abbott swept him out of the hall.

Catherine was alone in *her* house for the first time. It didn't exactly welcome her with outstretched arms, but neither did it repulse her; the thought that it might be waiting to make up its mind was unsatisfactory, even disturbing. The contents of Nicholas Tate's manila envelope were also open to question: a copy of his catalogue, listing every object of value at La Bastide. In most cases, and certainly when it came to Edward Walden's principal acquisitions, the price paid for each piece was given as well as its value at the time the catalogue had been compiled; this, Catherine discovered,

had been ten years before; Nicholas must have been
engaged in the task at the time of her childhood visit,
though he'd certainly given no indication of the fact and
had seemed to be pursuing pleasure as relentlessly as any
of the others. In any case he, or someone else, had been at
work on the matter more recently, because many of the
items, and again all the most important ones, had been
annotated in pencil: current valuation, with a neat
question-mark after each one. Even the most casual
glance revealed that the total ran into millions.

What was questionable was that Nicholas had not
asked whether the catalogue might possibly interest her,
he hadn't even left a civilized little note to say that he
didn't suppose it would; on the contrary, he had taken it
for granted that this was exactly what she wanted, both of
him and of La Bastide, and he was one hundred per cent
correct! She could regard his assessment as friendly
common sense or as sly insinuation, whichever she
preferred. At the moment, because it was less trouble,
and because she had more important things to think
about, she settled for the former, more kindly answer.

Using the catalogue much as a tourist uninterested in
painting might use a guide to the Louvre or the
Metropolitan, Catherine began to move from room to
room, inspecting only the objects which had earned a
maximum of noughts in the pencilled estimation. The
expression on her face might have interested and
surprised Monsieur Gosselin, but it wouldn't have
surprised Nicholas Tate. Gone was the quiet retiring
manner, the cool reserve; her expression was sharp with
acquisitive satisfaction, natural enough considering the
circumstances but none the less unexpected; she actually
hurried from Giotto to Guardi, Tabriz to T'sing, from
Famille Rose to Fragonard to Fabergé: hurried so fast
that she found herself quite dazed by so much prestigious
colour and magnificence—so many noughts.

It was a relief, after acting a part for Monsieur Gosselin, no less than for Madame Beaumont, Nicholas Tate, and even, in a different way, for lusty Jean-Michel, to be entirely herself for a little while. *This* was her reason for coming to France, to Montferrat. It was the thought of this Aladdin's cave which had made her heart seem to leap right out of her body as soon as the lawyer's voice, long distance, had said that Edward Walden was dead. The remembered face which had flashed across her mind, immediately, had not been that of her father but of Rembrandt's old woman at the foot of the stairs. There were, she had read, only a relatively small number of aunthenticated Rembrandts in the world, and she was about to possess one of them.

Jewels, jades, tapestries, Louis Quinze and Chippendale; no less than twelve great paintings for which every museum and gallery would be eager to bid, and twenty-two lesser masterpieces which would stand any auction-room on its head. Let old Natalia take what she had earned, let the legacies be counted out to lawyers and faithful servants and doctors and the rest of the rag-tag-and-bobtail! When all was paid and accounted for she, Catherine Grant Walden, was going to be a very, very, very rich woman.

And boy! did she know what to do with it! All that begging for affection, scrimping and saving any little leftover morsel of love; all those years of never knowing what man was going to be sitting at the end of the dining-room table opposite her mother, but knowing that he would only be nice to her because she was 'the daughter'; all that yearning for a father (the other girls had fathers) and that hunger for a place of her own which would be there next day, next year, all that deadly devouring instability — gone!

Of course she'd screwed up every relationship with every young man she'd ever known, demanding too much, more than the poor creatures had to give, forcing them into false moulds: father-figures but not absent, mother-figures but not drunk, big-brother-figures but not dead. How could any of them have survived? Doomed from the first meeting of eyes!

Well, it was over. The wise old French lawyer might be right, rich people might always be lonely, but not if they'd known what it was to be Catherine Walden, crushed between nullities. Very well, money couldn't buy happiness, or so they said, but who was asking for *happiness*, in God's name? something which only existed at fleeting and unexpected moments. And who was to say that those moments didn't come as often or as rarely to a rich person as to a poor one? Nobody, certainly not Catherine Walden. Certainly not 'Miss Asham by Thomas Gainsborough, 1771' (a great many noughts in the catalogue) whom she was at that moment inspecting. Miss Asham had been rich all right, witness those jewels, that dress, the Palladian palace in background, and Miss Asham looked happy enough; she was giving Miss Walden a sly smile which Miss Walden was able to return with confidence, in view of the fact . . .

Something outside the window had caught her eye. She gasped. The figure of a young man, apparently stark naked, moved across the terrace at the far end of the Italian garden; then disappeared. The glimpse seemed to have revealed very black hair and a certain familiar swagger of male assurance. But it couldn't be! Not here, not on *her* property!

With a patience which did her credit, she wasn't by nature a patient woman, Natalia Beaumont said, 'Paul, tell me this—why did you send for her, all the way from America? Did Edward ask it?'

'He . . . seemed to be asking it, yes. You know what it was like towards the end. He was confused, he

contradicted himself.' Monsieur Gosselin was also
confused, was also contradicting himself. He had retired
behind his desk as a defensive measure, and now felt
caged there, these two bright-eyed, bright-witted people
between him and the door which was his only means of
escape, short of a leap from the window.

'You could have asked my advice, I knew him better
than you did.'

'Natalia, one cannot ask advice on a legal matter from
an interested party.'

'Don't be pompous, my dear.'

'And I've refused all along the line to resort to this
fantastic guesswork you're all engaged in.'

Nicholas Tate said, 'Honestly, Paul, I don't think
Natalia's guessing.'

'I'm not.'

'You are, you both are. Everybody in this town is.
When David Rudd arrives tomorrow . . .'

Madame Beaumont leaned forward. 'Paul, Paul
darling, don't you see that it's *cruel* to leave it until then?'

'I see that legally it's the correct, the only thing to do.'

Madame threw up well-preserved hands, rings
flashing. 'If Nicky's right, and he usually is, she's up there
at La Bastide right now, counting all those damned
possessions like a child at Christmas, and none of them,
not one single solitary bauble, belongs to her or ever
will.'

'So you say, you have no proof.'

'Paul, I *know*. Edward told me more than once.'

'Frankly, Natalia, I don't believe it. Why would he do
such a thing?'

'Oh God!' said Nicholas, 'why did Edward do anything?
I expect he had reasons, probably good ones, knowing
him, but as usual he kept them to himself.'

'What you're suggesting isn't rational, it isn't even
decent.'

Natalia Beaumont snorted. 'Decent! You talk like an Englishman!'

Nicholas ignored this Gallic exchange. 'He couldn't stand his wife, Paul, I dare say the poor girl got lumped in with all that misery. Anyway "why" doesn't matter — the point is that you've got to . . . warn her at least. Anything else would be brutal, I agree with Natalia.'

'I'm sorry, I can't advise a client on a basis of pure conjecture, it's not correct.'

'Will you *stop* using that word!' Madame Beaumont stood up abruptly, her patience at an end. 'Nothing you've done so far has been in any way "correct". You shouldn't have sent for her, I'm sure Edward didn't want it. But you did. So the wretched child comes here, full of inflated dreams, and the first person to get his hands on her is that . . . that criminal moron, Pascal Lavallier, using *my* son's name.'

'Unfortunate, but as far as I'm concerned unavoidable.'

'Everything's avoidable, with a little forethought and common sense, a lawyer ought to know that!' She came and stood on the other side of the desk. Like all big men, Paul Gosselin wasn't used to being towered over, and didn't like it. 'You've got to explain things to her, warn her as Nicky said — the sooner the better. Yes, I know.' She forestalled his objections with a raised finger. 'It's not correct and at the moment there's no proof, but that's what you're going to do, Paul my dear, and we're here to see you do it.'

As Catherine came out of the house a cloud obscured the sun, the first time this had happened since her arrival at Montferrat. The sudden shadow was in some ways a relief, but it flattened the beauty of the garden, stole away its brilliance and, no doubt about it, introduced a subtle note of foreboding.

She had, up to this moment, been half-running, but

now she took a grip of herself; paused; sauntered forward, down the brick walk which led to the Italian garden, at the centre of which, her researches had told her, stood a fine 'Mercury' by Jean-Antoine Houdon, 1783.

The ring of ornamental ponds, plashing fountains, formal flowerbeds, appeared empty, and the only naked man to be seen was the winged god himself. As if admiring him, she circled the central pool where he stood, searching the walks which led away in artful false perspective beyond his lithe body. Nobody. It wasn't possible, was it, that she had imagined Jean-Michel? Certainly she had spent a good deal of her time thinking about him, not exactly reproving herself for having put a stop to their dalliance, but not in the least pleased with herself for having done so.

She turned into the alley of roses where she had walked with Natalia Beaumont. At the same moment the sun sailed out from behind the single cloud which punctuated a clear sky, and there he was, sitting on top of a stone plinth, his back against the hefty urn which topped it. He was smiling and not in fact naked, but wearing a pair of swimming-trunks which were, by design or accident (design she suspected), the same colour as his skin. The smile rekindled her anger. 'What in heaven's name are *you* doing here?' She had spoken in English.

He examined her face for a moment before replying, in French, 'I live here.'

She was absolutely flummoxed, and showed it, much to his amusement. 'What . . . what do you mean, you live here? Where? Why didn't you tell me?'

'People are crazy, always telling everything about themselves — Americans do it all the time. It leaves nothing to find out. No excitement, no mysteries.'

'All right, so you're mysterious! Jean-Michel, please tell me what you mean by "living here"?'

'Well . . .' He considered the question. He looked very fine, very young and vigourous up there on his plinth. Even in this irritating situation Catherine was unable to ignore the fact that he attracted her strongly; and she had rebuffed him because of some (possibly imagined) expression on his face!

He said carefully, 'Do you suppose Nicky Tate was your father's only boy-friend?'

They regarded each other in taut silence, he half-smiling, she considering his remark without revealing her thoughts — to his evident disappointment.

'You were my father's boy-friend, huh? So you live here.'

'Yes. He liked both, you know. Bisexual.'

'I see.'

'You don't believe me.'

'I'm perfectly prepared to believe he was bisexual, so many men are, but . . .' She shrugged, not completing the qualification.

'He liked them young. Nicky Tate's thirty-four.'

At this moment there was the sound of approaching footsteps. Neither the young man nor the girl moved, but she detected uneasiness in a flicker of his eyes. A buxom woman with black curly hair came into view, walking along a cross-path carrying a basket of peaches. She stopped on seeing the two of them and smiled at Catherine, a pretty, good-natured smile. 'Mademoiselle doesn't remember me.'

'Yes, of course I do. Madame . . . My father's house-keeper, Madame . . . Laval.'

'Not far off — Lavallier.' She showed the peaches. 'For your lunch, the first.' Then she looked up at the young man enthroned above them. 'What's my good-for-nothing son been telling you? Whatever it is, don't believe him. He's a terrible liar, aren't you, Pascal?'

'Terrible.'

The woman moved on, still smiling. Catherine was staring with wide, shocked eyes. 'Pascal! Madame Lavallier's son!'

'Yes. Don't worry, I was only kidding about being his boy-friend.' He slipped off his stone perch, but the girl was backing away from him. 'And you actually tried to . . . You're disgusting!'

He laughed, moving towards her. She evaded him furiously. 'Disgusting, perverted . . . !'

From laughter his expression changed abruptly to one of intense concentration. Their eyes met and held. Then she gave a little moan and turned, running away from him between the roses, petals whirling as she passed. For a long moment, a few seconds, he stood in exactly the same position, wearing exactly the same expression, almost as though he was listening to something far away. Then he swore under his breath and went after her.

He saw her disappearing around the tower; gave chase. Presumably she thought that he'd stayed where he was, because he came upon her suddenly, nearly fell over her. She was leaning against the ancient stonework, panting, still wild-eyed. As a matter of fact, not knowing or caring where she was going, the sudden drop from the terrace at the base of the tower to the rocks far below had taken her by surprise and stricken her with the old vertigo.

When he appeared she looked away from him. He examined her with different, sharper eyes. 'What did you mean . . . ?'

She cut him short savagely. 'I didn't mean anything, I was angry, I . . . Oh, go away!'

For answer he leaned against the hot stone beside her. To prevent further questions she demanded, 'Why did you pretend your name was Jean-Michel? Why the name of Madame Beaumont's son?'

'Because he'll be absolutely furious when he hears about it. Pompous bore!'

Coincidence, eh? She had been right to trust her instincts. Right in every respect. 'It wasn't chance that I gave you a lift.'

He shook his head. 'I saw you, from up here. Look!' He pointed. She could easily recognize the olive-trees where she had parked her car, the rock where she had leaned, examining La Bastide, remembering her visit all those years before.

'So I drove down to the village . . .'

'You have a car, then?'

'Yes, of course.'

She was staring at him now; shook her head in wonder. 'It was all planned.'

He nodded, pleased with his own cunning.

'Supposing there hadn't been a bus?'

'You'd probably have given me a lift anyway, or . . .' His gesture indicated that opportunities for the contriving of 'chance' encounters were limitless.

'So obviously you're not a student-farmer either.'

'I am in a way. Since I left school I've been helping with the estate here.'

Catherine was going over their short relationship in her mind, seeing how easily it had all fallen out according to his wishes. 'You like . . . playing games, don't you?'

'Yes.'

'Why?'

'It's interesting. And you learn more about people.' He was studying her intently. 'Don't you?'

She had never supposed that she would be pleased to see Abbott under any circumstances, let alone a circumstance as mildly compromising as the one she now found herself in: hiding around a corner with the nearly naked son of the housekeeper. Abbott showed no surprise and probably felt none. 'Your lunch is ready when you are, Miss.'

'Thank you, Abbott.'

'And Mr Tate rang. He said he was sorry not to leave you undisturbed all day as he promised, but would it be all right if he and Madame Beaumont came up with Monsieur Gosselin? He said there were things you ought to discuss.'

'Of course it's all right. When?'

'He said two-thirty, if you're agreeable. I'm to ring him back.'

'Fine — two-thirty.'

Abbott bowed and turned away. It said a good deal about him that he had not, by the flicker of those washed-out blue eyes, betrayed the fact that during this brief conversation he must have seen Pascal Lavallier slip quietly from her side; for when she turned back to him he had disappeared.

CHAPTER 7

Catherine ate slowly, lost in her thoughts. She drank only Perrier water; wine tended to make her sleepy in the afternoons, and something told her that on this particular afternoon she would need to be very wide awake indeed.

First of all she must gather her wits about her, and that meant dismissing Jean-Michel/Pascal from her mind altogether. It wasn't easy; the near-naked body kept darting in and out of the thoughts which she was trying to marshal into orderly ranks. There was also regret. For a few moments, sitting outside the shabby café (which, she now understood, he had chosen because he was little known there) she had experienced a moment of true happiness: the game of boule, the smiling country faces . . . And again at Lapalisse . . .

Well, she wasn't exactly unused to having small moments of happiness trampled underfoot; her mother

had possessed the trampling capabilities of a herd of
stampeding buffalo. And anyway, she had known within
a few minutes of meeting him, instinctively, that he was
not all he seemed, untrustworthy: too good-looking, too
self-assured, too conscious of himself.

So . . . She forced her mind to consider the impending
arrival of Madame Beaumont and Messieurs Tate and
Gosselin. Between the Vichyssoise and the lobster she
said, 'Abbott, how long has Madame Lavallier been
here?'

'More than twenty years, Miss, she started in the
kitchen.'

'Thank you.'

Between the lobster and the peaches she said, leafing
through the document in question, 'It must have taken
Mr Tate a long time to compile this catalogue—so
thorough!'

'Yes, Miss. Mr Tate was in and out for three or four
years. I seem to remember you meeting him on your
previous visit.'

'I did. Thank you, Abbott.'

A number of things were perfectly obvious; Madame
Beaumont had not gone to a meeting in Cannes, and
Nicholas Tate had never planned to be out all day; they
had both wanted to talk with Monsieur Gosselin and had
taken steps to ensure that she didn't know about it. She
had a reasonably accurate idea of the shape of things to
come; therefore her immediate problem was one of
attitude: which of many to adopt and how best to adopt
it?

They found her sitting in the shade with a book,
looking fresh and composed, and in every way at home.
Abbott appeared with coffee and liqueurs; met nobody's
eye; withdrew. Catherine looked at them expectantly,
grey eyes very clear and innocent. Monsieur Gosselin only
had to glance at the other two in order to realize, if he

hadn't before, that they were leaving it to him. He
cleared his throat. 'I'd like to say . . . As you know,
Mademoiselle, I've tried hard to present you with only the
facts, with what I know to be true. However, I've been . . .
prevailed upon to break that rule. Both Madame
Beaumont and Mr Tate feel that it's my . . . duty to
acquaint you with certain possibilities.'

'Really, Paul, I don't think . . .' To Madame
Beaumont's surprise the lawyer silenced her with a large
hand and continued his ponderous peroration: 'I want
you to know, in advance, that I still disapprove of this
recourse, but I do see that a case may be made for taking
it. I'm sorry, Natalia.'

Now that the moment had come, Madame Beaumont
glanced away indecisively. 'Is it better to be blunt or
diplomatic? Either way you're bound to be hurt.'

'I think,' said Catherine, 'I prefer bluntness — and I'm
quite used to being hurt.'

'Very well, I shall speak for myself first. As you know,
your father and I were lovers for a long time. I won't
pretend I didn't want him to marry me, I did. He
wouldn't. He said, "Once is enough, my dear,
particularly if the once was Laura." He grew to dislike
your mother very much indeed.'

'I wonder why he never divorced her.'

'Oh, obviously!' said Nicholas. 'As long as they were
married to each other they were in no danger of having to
marry anyone else. Edward never pretended otherwise,
not to me.'

'To me,' icily from the ex-mistress, 'he pretended
otherwise, for obvious reasons. Anyway, that's beside the
point. My son is his child.'

Catherine glanced away; then, her voice sounding
remote, diminished: 'Oh! I see. I didn't know.'

Natalia Beaumont felt like a murderess — a political
one perhaps, who believes that the end justifies the

means. Her face must have betrayed this because Monsieur Gosselin took up the woeful tale: 'But that isn't all, Mademoiselle. At a later date your father had an affair with his housekeeper, you may perhaps remember her?'

'Yes. I met her again this morning.'

'Madame Lavallier also bore him a son. I regret to say that this was the young man who assumed a false name and who . . . made your acquaintance so tortuously on the day you arrived here.'

'He must be insane!' She had managed not to say this to Pascal's face, for a variety of good reasons; it was a relief to say it now.

'I doubt if he's actually certifiable,' said Madame Beaumont evenly, 'but he gets up to some very odd things.' A sharper glance. 'He's an extremely attractive creature, I trust you didn't . . .'

'No!' Catherine sounded as severe as she felt. To any ordinary person his behaviour seemed altogether bizarre: immoral and irrational; but what did it seem to Pascal? And what exactly was it that she had glimpsed on his face by the reflection of passing headlights? Would he in fact have gone ahead if she had allowed it? With his own half-sister? Was there such a thing as half-incest?

'So you see,' said Monsieur Gosselin, 'Edward Walden fathered two illegitimate sons. As you said in my office, he was shattered by the death of your brother—we don't have to go into the psychological motivation, it doesn't concern us. Of course I could have told you this, I chose not to because I didn't think it had any bearing on the matter.' He shifted uneasily in his chair. 'Madame and Monsieur have convinced me otherwise—partially.'

Nicholas Tate sighed. 'We're beating about the bush. Catherine. What all this is leading up to . . . Oh God! Your father made a second will, and . . . and you and your mother were cut out of it altogether.'

Catherine stared at him blankly. Her elbow was resting on the arm of her chair; after a moment she raised a hand and put it over her eyes; sat there in silence with bowed head, fair hair falling forward. 'No!' she said at length. 'Oh *no!*'

She was remembering her walk among the roses with Madame Beaumont. 'How much has Paul Gosselin told you about the will?' Was this the true fulfilment of all those creeping doubts, the true meaning of her ignorance? Of course it had always been a lurking fear, but she had defied it, and must continue to defy it now; the alternative was too dreadful to consider.

Nicholas continued: 'I'm sorry. He told me and he told Natalia. We don't know about Marianne Lavallier, but I suppose he told her too.'

'You see,' said Monsieur Gosselin, 'this is where the guesswork begins — he told various people that he had made a second will.'

'Nonsense, Paul, we know he did.'

'Forgive me, Natalia, you don't know. He *said* he did, but that's another matter entirely, and as for Mademoiselle Catherine being cut out of it altogether, I've already told her where French law stands in this regard — it's extremely difficult to exclude one's own flesh and blood . . .'

'Paul,' interrupted Nicholas Tate wearily, 'Laura Walden agreed, years ago, to *renounce* any legal claim to her husband's estate.'

Catherine's voice came muffled from the bowed head: 'I can't believe that.'

'She did, your father told me. And after all she was a rich woman in her own right.'

'Not after all those men had finished with her.'

Paul Gosselin slapped his massive knee. 'We're still in the realms of hearsay.'

Natalia Beaumont stood up, again impatient. 'This is

intensely distasteful.' With a glare at the lawyer: 'It shouldn't have been allowed to happen. But it *has* happened and we must deal with it as best we can.' She looked down at the girl. 'All we're trying to do, my dear, is to soften the blow which must fall when David Rudd arrives tomorrow and reads the will. It would be insufferable for you to have to hear such things for the first time in, as it were, public.' She laid a delicate hand on the bowed shoulder. 'No good asking you to forgive us, not just now. I hope that in time you'll see that we had no option. Or that the alternatives were even more cruel.'

Catherine, still not looking up, said, 'I can . . . I can understand how he felt about Mother, but he had no reason to do such a thing to me.'

'I'm afraid he did it all the same. After various legacies, some of them very generous I'm sure, the estate is divided equally between five people: Madame Lavallier and her son, myself and my son, and . . .' She glanced at Nicholas Tate, clearly feeling that he had been silent for too long.

He grimaced. 'Catherine, did you know . . . ? I can't imagine your mother *not* telling you, plus gruesome details. Edward and I had a relationship for several years.'

'No, Mother never said anything.'

'Well we did, and I'm the fifth person mentioned in the will. It's the last thing I expected, he'd helped me enough already.'

'Insufferable!' said Madame Beaumont again; it wasn't easy to tell whether she was referring to the entire situation or merely to this more esoteric angle of it.

Silence fell. Catherine didn't move. After a time the older woman continued: 'Of course it's all very unfair. Nicky and I have discussed it, though not with Madame Lavallier, and in any case David Rudd will advise us — but obviously, once the estate is settled, we must each make you a voluntary gift . . .'

'*No!*' Catherine dropped her hand and stood up, eyes icy cold. 'I don't want any charity. If you're right, and I . . . I can't allow myself to think you are . . . Well, I managed all right in New York until this happened, and I'll go on managing—with my dreary job and my dreary apartment—I don't care, at least it's me, I know who I am. But *charity!*' She turned to Monsieur Gosselin who was staring at her with apprehensive astonishment. 'Thank you, Monsieur, you've been very kind and loyal, I'll never forget it.'

She wheeled away, and into the shadows of the house, glanced fiercely at the Rembrandt as she passed through the hall, emerged from soothing shade into incandescent heat, got into her stifling car, drove back to the Hôtel de la Poste, told Madame Albert that she had a headache, went up to her calm cool bedroom, and locked the door on the hot and contentious world.

Meanwhile at La Bastide Monsieur Gosselin was also leaving, having expressed an ironic hope that Madame Beaumont and Monsieur Tate were satisfied with what they'd insisted on doing.

'Paul, of course we are. You're the kindest of men, probably too kind for your own good, you can't tell me you'd have preferred all that to come out in front of Marianne and Pascal, and Abbott, and God knows who else?'

Not knowing the answer to this question, not even knowing whether it had any basis in truth, he shrugged; then took his leave and drove to the Café des Sports (he was in no mood for Julie) and played a game of chess with old Monsieur Forge; won it too.

Natalia, walking slowly through the Italian garden with Nicholas, said, 'It's so fortunate that you have all these contacts in the art world, everything will be so much easier.'

'I called Reisman at the Metropolitan, he agrees with

my valuation of the Giotto, give or take a few thousand. They're going to bid. I wonder if we could get the Italians, or maybe the Japanese, to push them up a bit.'

'Marianne agrees with us completely—did I tell you I had a long talk with her last night? Sell everything, pay the taxes, then divide what's left.'

'I'll probably try to buy some of the furniture myself—but that's my business, the principle remains the same.'

They walked in silence for a time, circling Houdon's Mercury, considering the gilded future; then Madame Beaumont said, 'I feel desperately sorry for that poor girl. I like her, she reminds me so much of Laura. She must be going through hell down there in that miserable little hotel. Do you think I ought to try and talk to her?'

'Wouldn't do any good, leave her alone. Later, this evening, I'll go myself—maybe take her out to dinner.'

'Oh Nicky, that would be kind.'

'If she doesn't refuse to see me!'

CHAPTER 8

Nicholas Tate was a little drunk by the time, seven o'clock, that he reached the Hôtel de la Poste. This had nothing to do with the awkwardness of his present mission, (he had embarked on many worse), and a great deal to do with the fact that he, almost alone among the people close to Edward Walden, or so it seemed, was genuinely upset by his death.

This surprised him, but then the whole relationship had been one of surprises, on both sides. He had considered Catherine's father to be a spoiled, self-centred sonofabitch, and had told him so on several occasions. At their parting, which had been acrimonious, he had missed the older man not at all, perhaps because he had known, deep down in his calculating mind, that Edward would always be there. And he'd been right: witness, among other things, the financial backing and therefore the success of his chosen career. But now Edward was no longer there, and it seemed that the calculating mind had, in fact, solved the wrong equation: $x + y$ did not add up to a hard-headed young businessman with a growing reputation; they added up to a deep and unexpected sense of loss.

He asked if he could speak to Miss Walden. Madame Albert, who knew a thing or two about *this* young man, make no mistake! was delighted to find herself onstage in Montferrat's great drama. She played him along for a while with the 'Mademoiselle-does-not-wish-to-be-disturbed' routine, but then allowed him to cajole her into calling Room 17 on the house-phone. To her surprise, and much more to Mr Tate's, Catherine said that of course she'd see him, would Madame Albert ask him to come up?

Nicholas found her lying on her bed, back to the window, face in shadow, so that he was unable to tell whether or not she'd been crying. Catherine, for her part, recognized the intoxication at once and roughly guaged its degree; she was an expert.

He said, 'I'm sorry, it's a lousy situation. Paul Gosselin should never have sent for you.'

'I'm glad he did.'

'That means you don't believe what Natalia and I said.'

She sat up on the bed, running both hands through her hair. 'How *can* I believe it? He couldn't have been so callous, so cruel.'

'Oh God! How many rich people have you known—really well?'

'Really well?' She shrugged. 'None.'

He spread both hands. 'They have entirely different

values, they don't even think the way we do. It's like
trying to make contact with . . . with something from
outer space—alien in every way.'

She shrugged again, apparently unconvinced. He
soldiered on. 'If you can have anything you want, do
anything you want, you lose all sense of proportion. You
can dimly understand that other people don't have very
much, long for better things and strive to get them,
but . . . it doesn't mean anything to you personally.'

'I simply don't believe that he'd cut his wife and
daughter right out of his will.'

'He'd already cut you both out of his *life*, for God's
sake! All right, it was a monstrous thing to do—however
awful your mother was he had no right to lump you in
with her—but Edward was always doing monstrous
things, and half the time he didn't even know it, he'd get
quite hurt if you told him.'

He went to the bed and sat down beside her. 'You've
got to understand, or you'll just go on suffering—that's
the effect he had on people. How do I make you
understand him? I need a drink, d'you suppose that bitch
would send us up a bottle of something?'

Watching him pace about her shadowed room, glass in
hand, Catherine realized that though he had indeed
come to see her out of compassion for her predicament he
was also driven by some urgent private need to explain
Edward Walden, not merely to her, perhaps not at all to
her, but to himself: all over again, presumably, since it
could hardly be the first time he had tried.

'It's a wonder he wasn't more of a mess, really. I mean,
look at that background! All that New England WASP
brainwashing, all those bushels of bloody money—his
mother was even richer than his father, wasn't she?—and
all those private schools and Harvard and balls in the
country and, my dear, a palace *in* New York!

'Catherine, for God's sake get off that bed and do

something about your face and hair, and let's get the hell out of this hell-hole, I bet that cow's got the whole place bugged!

'What I mean is, there wasn't a thing the poor sod could do about himself, he was set up from the cradle to the grave, everything lined with mink, even the coffin — as long as he behaved himself like a good boy. You see?'

'See what?'

'Oh come on, use your brains, you're got plenty. He made a *point* of misbehaving from the moment he first got the message — inherited wealth is the pits. Hark who's talking! Even my mother speaks to me now she knows I'm going to be rich . . .'

Once Catherine had thrown off the inertia which gripped her, she found the ensuing monologue, performed against a variety of unlikely backgrounds, enthralling if bizarre; it did much to augment her mother's purposely inaccurate version of Edward Walden's life. Moreover, it helped to fill the vacuum preceding the arrival of Mr David Rudd from London; her fears and thoughts were becoming repetitive, trotting interminably round and round her mind like horses in a circus.

On the drive to Toulon ('We'd better get out of Montferrat before they cook us with truffles and eat us.') he said, 'The trouble with people like Edward is they're constitutionally incapable — God! did I manage to say that? I must be sober — of taking anything seriously. They've never had to, there's no need. So the Matisse turns out to be a forgery? Good old Elmyr de Hory! Hang it in the servants' loo.' He looked at her to see if she was listening. Catherine, intent on a corkscrew road down the mountainside, merely nodded. And he had wanted to drive!

'I suppose it's better to be like that than one of those *concerned* rich people, all chic good causes and millionaire socialism because they're ashamed of their gold. Edward at least enjoyed his money, in so far as any rich person enjoys anything. He didn't rush around patronizing everyone in sight and blackmailing them with bequests, am I boring you?'

'Heavens no, I'm fascinated.'

'I know he wasn't all *that* rich, stinking with money of course but no Getty. It's the attitude, I mean take all that business with the Diplomatic Corps, what a farce! He didn't care if . . . Stop, Catherine, stop! There, that squalid-looking caff — we'll have a quickie. The son of the house has to be seen to be believed, Edward used to call him La Gioconda.'

'What happened in the Foreign Service? I never did understand.'

'Just as well, dear, not for the kiddies. He . . . Jesus, there's the son now! Don't look! Obese and spotty, thank God Edward can't see him. Where was I? Oh yes. By all accounts he came out of the army in a blaze of glory, Erroll Flynn couldn't have done it better. Quick refresher at Harvard Law School and straight into the service of Uncle Sam, what else would you expect with a family background like that? And one has to do *something* between games of tennis and the old bump and grind.'

'This was before he met Mother.'

Long before. And incidentally, take your uncle's advice — never trust good-looking men of thirty-seven who tell you that the idea of marriage has never entered their heads.'

'I never would.'

'Your mother did. Somebody that rich, that good-looking! Of course he was having a whale of a time, travelling the world as Uncle Sam's special rep. and bedding everything that came within reach, both sexes. It was bound to end in disaster.'

On the road again, he said, 'Mediterranean males blow

up just like that, don't they? Adonis today, Billy Bunter tomorrow.'

'Half the women too.'

'Yes. Marianne Lavallier was an absolute raving beauty when I first saw her. I always thought Edward was a prime prick to have it off with his own housekeeper, but I think he found it all rather different and *French*, François Mauriac country. Now she's fat, and her bouncing boy will be just the same, evil little sod! Did he try to make you?'

'Sort of.'

'I thought so. Incest would be something new, wouldn't it? He's got a lot of his Dad in him, that one. Where was I?'

'Leaving the Foreign Service.'

'Well, first of all he married Mummy. *More* bloody money! And by all accounts the Wedding of the Century, in Paris of course, with Natalia overplaying Chief Bridesmaid in yards of chartreuse wild silk, I bet she looked divine, even if she does say so herself, and Mummy in a cloud of white, what a performance!

'It was about . . . two or three years later. She'd had your brother, I don't think you were on the way yet, I'm not quite sure. Anyway, they were in Rome, Edward was First Secretary by then. That's all Uncle Sam needed! His Roman First Secretary caught with his pants down in the company of some toothsome moppet from the French Embassy.'

'Male or female?'

'Oh male — female wouldn't have mattered. Something alluring in the Military Attaché's department, Edward always had a soft spot for a well-fitting uniform. And of course he *would* choose a Frenchman at a time when the Yanks and the Froggies weren't speaking!

'So then we have a big scandal and he gets thrown out. Serve him bloody well right for having no discretion, but who needs discretion when they've got that much loot? Your mother took it on the chin like the Upper English lady she was, you've got to hand it to her. But it must have been a mortifying experience in those days, before every Tom, Dick and Harry came out of the closet and started marching up and down with placards, Gay Rights, Gay Lib, all the rest of the ballsaching crap.

'I don't think she ever forgave him, and I'm damn sure she never trusted him again. He laughed, of course.

'It must have been about now that your brother died and you were born. Poor love, you couldn't have arrived at a worse moment, could you? I'm surprised you managed to grow up at all, let alone sane and beautiful to look at. As far as I can make out, they were both beside themselves with grief.'

In a bar overlooking the harbour at Toulon, he said, 'Edward went off to Kashmir on his own. Selfish thing to do, of course, but I suppose the marriage was on the rocks anyway. When he got back he found your mother had fitted herself up with a kosher, one hundred per cent hetero lover.'

Catherine nodded. 'That would have been the first love-of-her-life.'

Nicholas stared into his glass. He was passing into a glum stage. Catherine hoped that it would be short-lived.

'But you see I'm not doing Edward justice. I loved him, he really was a lovely lovable man in lots of ways. Ruined by too much money. He could be so . . . good, thoughtful, generous — most rich people aren't generous, but he was. He could also be an absolute bastard, and I'm not sure he ever knew the difference. Just as he had no idea of the value of money, he had no idea of his own value. He used to say, "Nicky, stop worrying, it doesn't matter. We're all spots of fly-shit on the celestial windowpane. One of these days the heavenly window-cleaner will wipe us off." '

In another bar, full of sailors at whom he stared with morose interest: 'Okay, Mummy and Daddy drifted apart. He tried London for a while, and it bored him. So he came to La Belle France and, surprise, surprise! Who should be waiting for him at Cherbourg under her smart little parapluie but Madame Natalia Beaumont, a widow of independent means and *extra*ordinary determination. I rather fancy the blond number in the corner, don't you? Only in theory, sailors are a bore and with French ones you get the Gauloises and the garlic thrown in.'

Later, over perfectly cooked fish in a cellar-restaurant thick with fishermen and the smoke of grilling, he cheered up considerably. 'In fact, I think Natalia was the best thing that happened to your father — apart from me. I don't think she ever loved him, which I did, but then she was thirty and I was twenty-three — she'd been married to some tiresome Frenchman and I hadn't — she was Franco-Russian, very cosmopolitan, I was East Grinstead, very suburban. My father's an antique-dealer, by the way, hard graft in the blood!

'Natalia's a worker. She made him happy because she worked at it. He wanted a son, she bloody well gave him a son — by the way, why did he always blame your mother because your brother died?'

'I didn't even know he did.'

'Oh yes, in some way it was all her fault — or he thought it was, which comes to the same thing.'

'Is that why he was . . . against *me*?'

'It'd make a tidy little psychological parcel, wouldn't it? But . . . no, I don't think so, you just got lumped in with her. And he was a bit put off when you visited him that time, no daughter of *his* could possibly be fat and awkward. If he could see you now he'd change his mind double-quick — rather an artistic snob, our Edward. What about this fish? Best restaurant in the South of France, and only the local workers ever come here. Oh yes, Natalia's as bright as a button, she knew that the thing he valued most was someone he could trust — they feel they can't trust anyone, you see.'

'Then what happened? Why Marianne Lavallier?'

'That's the crazy thing, all that intelligence, female cunning, you name it, and Natalia played her hand wrong. Mind you, I can see why — she knew about the death of your brother, she knew it was one of the few *real* things that ever happened to him — he couldn't laugh that one off, or buy him back, he couldn't even get your mother to make him a new one because by that time they weren't speaking.

'So you can't blame Natalia for thinking her baby boy was the Ace. She really did believe Edward was going to marry her, and I think she put on a bit of pressure. Big mistake! He'd *had* marriage up to the eyeballs, and all she did was drive him away, straight into the arms of pretty, dopey Marianne, all big tits and peasant guile. You didn't find *her* talking about marriage when Pascal appeared on the scene, oh dear me no! She knew her place and exactly what it was worth. Just watch it all pay off tomorrow when David Rudd reads that will.' And, seeing the expression on her face: 'Sorry! But this is a lesson in reality, we all have to live with it.'

'But the two boys — didn't he . . . love either of them?'

'Not really, he wasn't interested. Having them was like buying the Rembrandt. In the heat of the moment they both seemed to prove something — God knows what, he knew he had a pair of balls and a lot of money — but once he'd got them he found they didn't prove anything, back to Square One. Mind you, he was as pleased as pie when he saw what a beautiful object young Pascal was growing up to be.'

'Not much fun for Pascal!' Whichever way she turned, she seemed to find a fellow-feeling for that odd half-brother, though it was a long way from strong sexual attraction to the knowledge that they had both, in their different ways, been discarded by the same father. 'No wonder he's a bit weird.'

'Weird! He's a nut-case—but not as bad as Natalia's dashing Lieutenant, you haven't met him yet, have you?'

'No.'

'You may be saved. He's learning to jump out of aeroplanes; with any luck his parachute won't open.'

'He can't be that bad.'

'Oh, he is, he is!' The bright eyes, more than a little out of focus, were turned upon her. 'Dreadful little snob, too. I mean, he could understand Edward having it off with his lovely aristocratic mother, all those supposed Russian counts in the background, and producing lovely Jean-Michel—but to pass her up in favour of his own *housekeeper*, my dear, a mere *peasant* . . . ! He and Pascal loathe each other's guts.'

'That's why Pascal used his name, with me.'

'Of course. The dashing lieutenant hit the fan when Mother told him about it on the phone. Pascal will never be forgiven.'

'He does sound pretty awful.'

'He's the *pits!* He never came to the funeral, of course—one doesn't actually acknowledge that one's a little bastard, I mean none of one's brother officers know, it simply isn't done. But I bet you any old odds that he appears for the reading of the will.'

'You're kidding.'

'Oh no I'm not, you don't know what the Grandes Écoles do to them—Polytechnique in his case, naturally. He's a po-faced little crypto-fascist brim-full of bullshit!'

Back in the car and on the road to Montferrat, now fuddled by sleepiness as well as by drink, he said, 'Anyway, to return to the subject of tonight's lecture— following Marianne and the appearance of dear little Pascal screaming his head off, the big pendulum swings again and suddenly the Master is tired of tits and babies. Enter Master Nicholas Tate of East Grinstead, taking a nice holiday in the South of France ooh-là-là!'

He was silent. Catherine thought that he must have fallen asleep, but he was staring at the road ahead as if hypnotized by the headlights. 'Where did you meet?'

'A perfectly gruesome gay bar in Saint Tropez, but then they're all gruesome, aren't they? I was pissed, game for anything, regained consciousness in what seemed to be a reasonably smart bedroom somewhere up in the hills. I imagine my face was, as they say, a picture when I finally made it downstairs with a dreadful hangover and found myself looking at Gainsborough and Giotto and all the rest of it.'

'There's another thing, another reason rich people have no values. They can never *ever* know, deep down inside, whether the pretty little object picked up in a bar is really fond of them, even attracted to them, or just latching on to the goodies. What's more, one's never quite sure oneself.'

'But you were together for years.'

'Five.'

'What did Madame Beaumont think about that?'

'I told you, she's as bright as a button. Edward could hardly use *me* as a hostess for all that endless entertaining, sitting at the other end of the table in pink chiffon! But Natalia was always there, woman of the world, boys will be boys, "you do Edward so much *good*, chéri", biding her time. She's eternal, I'm just a one night stand.'

'Five years?'

'Okay, a five year stand.'

'You certainly made yourself useful, that catalogue's a masterpiece.'

'Dead easy. And I got to meet all the right people, didn't I? So by the time I took off on my own, financed by

Edward, I was as bold as brass and thought I knew everything, pretentious little bastard!'

'Madame Beaumont said you were doing very well.'

'Yes, I am, thanks to him.' He shook his head. 'I'll tell you a funny thing—Edward only *really* understood how fond of him I was when I said I was bored and I'd met someone younger and prettier, without a penny to his name, and I was buggering off. It was only then that he realized just why I'd stuck around so long, and it was only then, when I'd gone, that he realized he missed me.'

'Ah,' she said, 'hence all that business about your old room being kept for you.'

'Sure, hence that. And of course remembering me in his will, which God knows I never expected, he'd been generous enough already. It's so bloody sad, isn't it? If you're rich you only know what you've got when you haven't got it any longer. I think that's why I hit the bottle this evening—so bloody sad!'

When they finally came to a stop in front of La Bastide, austere by moonlight, Catherine said, 'I wonder if Abbott's waiting up for you.'

'Oh yes. The creep!'

'My father seemed to like him.'

Every rich man has to have an Abbott, or a whole crowd of Abbotts. He was loyal, he held things together; if anybody's a diplomat it's Abbott. I've seen him save sinking dinner-parties, defuse drunks, pay off the rough trade, terrify the media, there's nothing I haven't seen him do. Whatever's in the kitty for him, he's earned it.' And looking at her blearily: 'I tried to explain why you got cut out of the will with Mummy and I made a balls-up, I haven't explained a dicky-bird.'

'You have—in a way.'

'Too late now, the Wisdom evades me, I'm about to pass out. I'd better pop into bed before that police-dog gets my leg for a late snack.' He leaned over and kissed her more or less on the cheek for which he was aiming. 'If Mama Natalia or I are stupid enough to offer any more charity, grab it!'

Catherine shook her head.

'That makes you a dumb cow.'

'So I'm a dumb cow.'

He levered himself out of the car and achieved a form of independent balance. 'You're a nice girl and you're beautiful. Forget the bloody will, you aren't included, go and find yourself a lovely rich man and marry him.'

'I'll think about it.'

'Not only a dumb cow but an *obstinate* dumb cow!'

'Correct.'

Glancing in the rear-mirror as she drove away, she observed that he had indeed been apprehended by one of Inspector Mattei's men, the Doberman threatening to pull him off his feet. Nicholas was waving his arms about and shouting. An ugly situation might well develop, but doubtless Abbott would materialize and deal with it.

PART TWO

I wish it, I command it. Let my will take the place of reason.

JUVENAL

CHAPTER 1

Monsieur Gosselin collected Catherine from the hotel and drove her up to La Bastide for the reading of the will. Abbott, suitably grave, opened the door to reveal David Rudd waiting for them in the hall, Rembrandt's old lady peering rheumily over his shoulder. He was a slender, alert man, full of well-rehearsed charm, boyish in his middle fifties. A lock of sandy hair fell over his forehead, and he was forever pushing it aside as if irritated by it; but he managed to get away with this affected habit just as he got away with that particularly English untidiness of dress which contrives to be distinguished, but only just. 'I'm so sorry, Miss Walden, we had no record of your new address.'

'Hardly new, I've had the apartment for two years.'

'When we called New York you'd already left.' He tried a charming but hesitant smile.

Catherine remained unimpressed. 'Luckily Monsieur Gosselin was better informed.'

'He had the advantage of being near to your father.'

She shrugged. Abbott ushered them towards the library where the others were waiting. To palliate Catherine's evident irritation, Monsieur Gosselin asked all the correct questions about his British colleague's wife. It seemed that the operation had gone reasonably well, though it was still too early for the specialists to form an exact opinion.

At the door of the cool, book-lined room they were greeted by a tableau of almost comical solemnity. Sargent, giving rein to his habitually repressed humour, might have enjoyed painting it: the surroundings so rich, the chosen clothing so sombre, as if the funeral had only

just taken place instead of having been concluded days
before.

Natalia Beaumont and Nicholas Tate, hung-over,
wore grey lightened by touches of discreet colour, his tie,
the rose at her breast, but the Lavalliers had settled for
peasant black in which both of them looked remarkably
handsome, even aristocratic. A newcomer, erect in
uniform, could only have been Jean-Michel Beaumont,
wrenching himself away from his duties, as Nicholas had
been willing to bet that he would, in order to attend this
division of the spoils. With his neat fair hair, powerful
physique, scrubbed good looks — very like his father's — he
was the prototype young and ambitious army officer, just
unremarkable enough to be a success. He was standing at
attention.

Catherine could barely recognize him as her tormentor
of ten years before, and he had obviously forgotten all
about it, giving her a stiff little bow, no smile. The only
other member of the gathering was a grey-haired man
with a military moustache and a vinous nose: the local
doctor, Sarazin by name, who had attended Edward
Walden, as well as various stricken guests, for more than
twenty years.

Overall there was an atmosphere of extreme tension,
principally occasioned by the fact that ten minutes before
Catherine's arrival the two half-brothers had actually
come to blows, smashing a valuable T'sung vase in the
process. The bone of contention, naturally enough, had
been Pascal's use of Lieutenant Beaumont's name during
his brief, and considering their blood relationship,
scandalous pursuit of Catherine. In fact the skirmish had
not come to much and had been broken up by Abbott
with his customary aplomb. However, Pascal had
succeeded in landing a satisfactory punch in his
opponent's abdomen, knocking the wind out of him with
the usual humiliating results. Jean-Michel was still

nursing his grievance, Pascal was pleased with himself, the respective mothers were ignoring each other's presence.

Of course Catherine was aware of the charged atmosphere but attributed it to the huge fortune which they all knew to be at stake. Avoiding eyes, Pascal's in particular, she sat down on a leather sofa slightly apart from the others and drew Monsieur Gosselin on to it beside her. Abbott took up position in the background, correctly inferior but looming.

David Rudd opened his briefcase and produced from it a large envelope. Every eye in the room followed his unhurried fingers as they tore it open and extracted from it several sheets of heavy paper. So intense was the burning interest focused upon this document that it might well have yielded to instantaneous combustion, bursting into flames in his hands. A pause. He had forgotten his glasses; found them; balanced them on his long nose and gave them all a schoolmasterish look over the top of the frames as if to make sure that they were properly attentive. Properly attentive!

He cleared his throat. ' "I, Edward Grant Walden, being in good health and of sound mind . . ." '

It was not in fact a very long document, and there were no preliminary and minor legacies. Edward Grant Walden had bequeathed his entire estate, money as well as possessions, to his wife, Laura, and upon her decease to the children of their marriage. That was all.

The silence which followed was solid enough to have been cut in slices and handed around on plates like rich and indigestible cake. David Rudd continued: Edward Grant Walden had been mindful of the fact that at the time of his death various dependants and retainers would deserve consideration, but he was fully confident that such matters could be left to the generosity and good sense of the beneficiaries and advisers.

With lawyer-like redundance he added, 'I need hardly explain that since Laura Walden is dead, as is the only son, Matthew, this means that the estate in its entirety goes to the surviving child, Catherine.'

Nothing else? It was an unspoken but resounding cry in that petrified silence. Mr Rudd answered it by folding up the document carefully.

Monsieur Gosselin put a large hand over Catherine's for a second; she nodded without raising her eyes from the pattern of the Persian carpet. The Beaumonts and the Lavalliers, mothers and sons, were still reeling from the impact, unable to regain their balance. Madame Beaumont was the first to find a cobwebby voice: 'The . . . date of the will was . . .'

David Rudd unfolded the document again and repeated the date upon which Edward Grant Walden had signed this deadly testament.

'But that's . . . twenty-five years ago.'

Nicholas Tate, who knew better than anyone else what she had had to put up with in order to earn this straight left to the jaw, was also regaining his faculties: 'I think . . . it was generally thought . . . that Edward made another will, much later, twenty or more years later.'

The lawyer nodded, took off his glasses and pushed back that troublesome lock of hair. 'Yes, he talked about it, many times, but whenever I suggested that we actually get down to brass tacks and draw it up, he . . . seemed to shy away from the subject.'

In spite of professional prudence, Monsieur Gosselin could not resist saying, quietly, 'So much for guesswork and gossip!'

Natalia Beaumont had aged ten years in as many minutes. She said, 'But he *told* me . . .' She turned her head, with evident difficulty, and looked at Marianne Lavallier, who nodded. 'Yes, I too always understood . . .'

Monsieur Gosselin's deep sigh dismissed the folly of

such 'understanding', and Lieutenant Beaumont began
to shout: 'This is absurd, ridiculous. We all knew . . . we
all *know* . . . Mr Rudd, are you sure?'

'My dear boy, of course I'm sure. One doesn't make
mistakes about wills, overlook them, forget them — what
do you mean?'

The Lieutenant could not explain what he meant.
Nicholas Tate, head splitting from this assault following
too many mixed drinks, knew from business experience
how touchy legal men were apt to be: 'We're not
questioning your professional integrity, David.'

'I should hope not. If lawyers were held accountable for
all the idiosyncrasies of their clients . . .' He waved this
absurd idea aside, and added more calmly: 'As you all
know, I came here many times over the years. Edward
was perfectly happy to discuss his investments, bonds, all
that kind of thing — in fact, being an American, he was
very knowledgeable about them. And he always *talked*
about making another will, but he kept putting it off.
One knows from experience that the older people get, the
less they like to think about dying. I mentioned it to him
again when I last saw him, during the winter. He was ill,
but his mind was as sharp as a razor. He said, "Don't
bully me, David, I'm thinking about it." '

The silence came surging back to engulf them, heavier
for these deadening revelations: Edward Walden had
been 'thinking about it', but he had not cared enough for
any of them to turn his thoughts into action.

Catherine was still lost in contemplation of the carpet.
The little doctor looked as though he would rather be
elsewhere: in the nearest bar, most probably. Abbott
remained still and silent in the background, only his pale
blue eyes moving. There now emerged, quietly at first, a
shocking, a sacrilegious sound, repressed but unsuccess-
fully and growing louder: laughter: spurts of laughter
which could not have been more shocking had they

been spurts of blood.

'*Pascal!*'

'I . . . I'm sorry. Oh God, your . . . your *faces!*'

Natalia Beaumont was on her feet, blazing: 'You appalling . . . nauseating . . .'

Her son moved forward purposefully, fists again clenched, but the little doctor grabbed his arm and held it with surprising strength and authority. Marianne Lavallier took over: 'Pascal, leave the room at once. *At once!*'

Her son stood there, dark eyes glittering with tears of mirth, laughter bubbling out of him uncontrollably. He wiped the eyes on his sleeve, stepped up to the sofa, bent down and kissed Catherine on the cheek; then reeled away towards the door, still convulsed.

The sound of his monstrous merriment dwindled away. A door slammed. Suddenly they were all talking at once. Madame Beaumont said, 'There must be some mistake . . .'

'Natalia, *how* can there be a mistake?'

'But he told me.'

'He told me too, shortly after Pascal was born — he said, "Both you and your son . . ." '

'When I decided to join the army he said he was very proud of me, and I needn't worry about . . .'

'. . . and of course I was surprised, he's already been so generous, but I can remember his exact words . . .'

'Nicholas, everybody talks, they don't always do anything about it.'

'I have repeatedly said that one cannot make hearsay the basis for . . .'

Quite suddenly Catherine, who had neither moved nor spoken, nor indeed looked at any of them, stood up and turned to face them, grey eyes very direct. They fell silent, staring, as if they'd forgotten her presence and were surprised to see her there. She said, 'I think we ought to . . . to pause for a moment. This has been a shock for us all. Perhaps . . .' She looked at Abbott, 'Something to drink, some coffee. We need a little time to pull ourselves together.'

This practicality altered all balances. Abbott bowed, and when Catherine headed for the door, made haste to open it for her. Monsieur Gosselin followed her out into the hall. To Abbott, Catherine said, 'I know how much my father depended on you, how fond of you he was. We'll come to an arrangement you won't regret.'

'Thank you, Madam.' She noticed how, on the instant, she had been upgraded. She turned to Monsieur Gosselin. 'You were right, weren't you?'

'I cannot tell you how I abominate gossip. We shall have a thousand things to discuss with David Rudd.' He glanced over his shoulder into the library where Mr Rudd, cornered, was nodding lugubriously in answer to a passionate tirade from Lieutenant Beaumont. 'I doubt if he'll be able to give us his attention until . . .'

'I don't want to talk now anyway. I . . . To be honest, I'm not feeling too great, I'd like a little air.'

Of course he was prepared to accompany her, but she laid a hand on his arm and smiled. He nodded. 'Mademoiselle naturally wants to be alone.'

'For a few minutes.'

She walked out into the garden. The mid-morning heat was oppressive, not even the faintest stirring of a breeze. Statues as well as flowers seemed to droop, and from this distance the fountains in the Italian garden could have been disgorging molten metal. Catherine took the path leading to the tower, thinking that on that wide circular terrace overlooking so many miles of open countryside she might find a breath of wind.

It would have been inhuman not to have felt satisfaction; now, away from them all, she could show it in a small, private smile of triumph. But she didn't find cooler air. Heat blazed back at her from the massive stones, and the valley lay shimmering into clear distance, every rock and tree harshly delineated. Even the cicadas seemed daunted.

She ventured closer to the low wall edging the terrace, hoping to catch a breeze there, but all she caught was the old stomach-churning insecurity imparted by heights.

'Well,' said Pascal, 'congratulations!'

She had not realized until this moment, standing so near this dizzying drop, that she was a little afraid of him. He had pulled down his neat tie, and the best black suit now made him look merely raffish. He noticed her reaction at once. 'What's the matter? Did I scare you?'

'No. I'm . . . silly about heights.'

'Oh yes. That stupid Jean-Michel used to tease you, didn't he? — that time you came to stay.'

'You remember? It's funny, I don't remember you at all.'

'I was kept in the background.' He grimaced. 'But there wasn't much I missed.'

During this, he had taken her arm, leading her across the terrace, out of the bludgeoning sunlight and into the shade of the bougainvillæa from which he had first examined her through Edward Walden's powerful binoculars. They then regarded each other intently. Was it, Catherine wondered, their sibling blood that seemed to make them understand each other so well? Because, no doubt about it, and as experience had already proved, an instinctive understanding certainly existed between them.

'You shouldn't have laughed, it was an awful thing to do.'

'But it was so *funny!*'

'You think it's funny to be cut out of your father's will, completely, just like that?'

'Of course. Money's a bore. All the people who used to come here, all the things they did and said, all this greedy calculation since he died—boring, boring!'

She shook her head. 'What an odd person you are!'

'That makes two of us.' So he also felt it; but what exactly did he mean? Before she could ask him he grasped her firmly by both forearms, pulled her against him and was kissing her hard. She fought back, but he had foreseen that and he was strong. Then, motivated no doubt by what had just taken place in the library, she stopped struggling and opened her mouth to him. He pushed her back against the brilliant shower of bougainvillaea, thrusting at her. She wasn't in the least surprised to feel that he was sexually aroused. If there had been a bed handy they might well have fallen upon it there and then, and their entire relationship, already so complex and to become more so, would have been changed.

But there was no bed, and somebody might appear around the corner at any moment, as Abbott had appeared on a previous occasion. Only after this thought had crossed her mind did she remember that in any case he was her half-brother. The heady moment of desire, unexpected physical counterpart of what she had experienced mentally upon hearing the contents of her father's will, was extinguished. She sagged in his arms, no longer pushing against him, and laid her head against his chest.

'Okay,' he said, 'when?'

'Oh Pascal! Obviously, never.'

'Obviously my arse!'

'Obviously. Please let go of me, somebody might see.'

'You want to.'

Not much good denying that now. 'Yes.'

'Then why not? We aren't going to make babies.'

She disentangled herself and moved away. 'Pascal, it's called incest.'

'It could just as well be called bouillabaisse—who cares?'

She turned and gave him a long, cool look, her heart sinking. What had Monsieur Gosselin said about rich people? 'I think they find it difficult to make friends, they're too suspicious.' She was rich now, and she was indeed suspicious. But that was nonsense; moreover, she had never trusted this young man from the beginning, and she'd better not forget it.

'What are you thinking?'

At least she could afford to be honest with him; he probably knew her thoughts anyway. 'About your motives.'

He laughed; leaned back against the bougainvillaea, laughing, and it struck her that the riotous creeper was no more vivid than he was. Even while her immediate desire for him diminished, her consciousness of that desire increased. And she hated his laughter. 'They'll be waiting for me, I must go in.'

'Not,' he said, 'with bits of bougainvillaea all over the back of your dress.' And, as on a previous occasion, he began to brush her down: rather harder than necessary, obviously enjoying the physical contact as much as the opportunity for mild chastisement.

'Please,' she said, 'stop laughing, there's nothing to laugh about.'

'How can you say such a thing? Particularly when you've just met our lovely half-brother for the first time! There's always something to laugh about.'

Lieutenant Beaumont had drawn his mother out into the garden, away from the salon where Abbott had seen fit to serve refreshment: though there seemed little reason for his choosing this particular room unless it was his idea of a joke to surround certain people with some of the more choice worldly goods which had just slipped between their fingers.

Jean-Michel, circling the swimming-pool, was in a

ferment: 'This is appalling, what are we going to do?'

'I shall take legal advice, of course.'

'We all *know* he made another will.'

'We don't know, my dear, I wish we did.'

'I've only got twenty-four hours' leave. I shall ask for an extension right away, you need me here.'

'That's not necessary, not at the moment. Legal matters take time.'

'Time! That wretched girl will have sold the place and everything in it. By God, I'd like to throw her out and send her packing, right back to America where she belongs!'

If Natalia Beaumont was honest with herself about her son, never an easy procedure, she had to admit that this over-excitement and this intention of getting extended leave immediately didn't do him a great deal of credit. It had proved perfectly convenient for him to be unable to get leave in order to attend his father's funeral; indeed, he had accepted Edward Walden's death phlegmatically, to say the least! She thought his anger was stupid, but then she had long since grown used to the idea that he was not the brightest of boys; any child conceived by herself and Edward Walden ought to have more brain—though of course with those American families one never knew what lay behind the façade, nor how close to it! Mother-like, she also thought that anger made him look very young and handsome. She said, 'Jean, listen to me. I'm not a fool and I'm a businesswoman. I have an excellent lawyer in Marseille who'll tell me exactly where we all stand.'

'I bet she found the proper will and burned it.'

'Now you're being childish, dear, wills aren't left lying about, this one was in a safe in London. The first thing to do is make sure of our legal rights. If any.'

'*If any!* But you know as well as I do . . .'

Madame Beaumont let the storm blow. She had

learned from experience that it was the best way. If only
he had taken after Edward, insouciant and dismissive,
but alas, emotionally he was a facsimile of her own
grandfather on her mother's side, who had been able to
work himself up into a real Russian frenzy, often with the
aid of a glass or two of vodka, usually terminating the
display with a torrent of real Russian tears. In her
moments of greatest doubt she wondered whether her
volatile boy would acquit himself well, even adequately,
on the field of battle, if chance ever happened to lead him
to it. She had to accept the consoling thought that he was
probably the kind of officer who would act with insane
bravery, thus earning decorations as well as promotion.

'. . . and I'm not only thinking of myself, I'm thinking
of you. I'd always planned that when we got the money
you could give up your work . . .'

'But I love my work, I'd be bored stiff without it.'

'Not that I mind you being "in trade" as some of the
chaps would call it. I don't think that way and I'm not a
snob, thank God!'

'No, of course you're not.'

'But running a chain of shops—it simply isn't your
style.'

'Jean-Michel, I enjoy . . .'

'I've always wanted you to have an easy, gracious
life—and now this *disaster!*'

His mother knew that the storm, unchecked, might
blow for a very long time: longer than her patience could
bear. 'Jean, we ought to go back. The others will think it
strange, bad-mannered . . .' She knew that above all
things he abhorred the idea of being thought strange or
bad-mannered. He subsided at once, bottling up his
rancour for another time, and followed her like a lamb.

As soon as Catherine rejoined them she knew that the
situation had crystallized itself: the surface attitudes

which they were all going to adopt as well as the underlying hostility. Sides had been taken and the line of battle drawn up, as expected: Madame Beaumont and the glowering Lieutenant, Nicholas Tate and Marianne Lavallier, against herself and supporting lawyers. Where Abbott stood was not particularly important (or so she thought—it was to prove a dire miscalculation), he could expect a handsome reward either way. Only absent Pascal occupied, as ever, an ambiguous position and was not, as ever, to be trusted. The little doctor had disappeared, with relief no doubt, and was probably at this moment downing a well-earned pastis.

As a signal of her public posture, Madame Natalia even managed a smile. 'You were quite right, my dear. A civilizing pause—none of us quite ourselves.' She became aware of the fact that she was holding a glass of the champagne which her late ungrateful lover had so much enjoyed at this time of the morning. 'You haven't got a glass.' Out of long habitude of being the hostess here she looked about for Abbott, but Catherine was there first. 'I'd like a Bourbon on the rocks, please, Abbott.'

'Yes, Madam.'

The exchange told everybody, very concisely, all that there was to know, including as it did the initial airing of Abbott's 'Madam'.

Catherine said, 'It was very wrong of my father to . . . mislead you all, but then he seems to have been like that.' She smiled at Nicholas, who was already, she could tell, regretting his alcoholically-inspired biography of the night before. 'Knowing him as well as you all did—' the grey eyes moved from mistress to boy-friend to mistress—'I'm surprised that you believed him. I certainly wouldn't have done so, but then . . .' She shrugged, dismissing the lack of interest which Edward Walden had always shown in his daughter.

Nicholas now unveiled the public attitude which he

intended to adopt. 'I'm disappointed, of course, no point in being hypocritical, but nobody's congratulated you on your . . .' He had been going to say 'luck', but something in the grey eyes cautioned him, and he made do with ' . . . your inheritance.'

Madame Beaumont nodded absently; neither she nor Marianne Lavallier were about to resort to British standards of fair play, however false. Jean-Michel remained mutinously silent, no doubt about *his* feelings!

Catherine thanked Nicholas, and added, 'I know I was ungrateful, perhaps a bit silly and rude too, when you and Madame Beaumont so generously offered . . .' She turned to the two lawyers who were talking quietly together under the Degas. 'Mr Rudd, please help me. I'm trying to tell our friends that I feel bound . . . I want very much to make some kind of financial arrangement. The will requested that, didn't it?'

'Not of course in so many words, the decision was left to the discretion of the beneficiaries.'

'And their legal advisers.'

'Yes.'

She looked at Natalia Beaumont who was having difficulty in swallowing the pill of charity, but was not, like Catherine herself, actually going to refuse it in case it happened to be the only available cure. On the other hand she could see that her son was bursting with refusal, for fatuous reasons of 'honour' no doubt; she silenced him with a ferocious look. Madame Lavallier, a practical French peasant, would take anything which might come her way. Nicholas Tate had not made good in a cut-throat profession by speaking out of turn.

Catherine continued, 'I don't want to talk about it just now. I . . . I remember too well how I felt when you told *me* that my father had excluded me altogether.'

Neither Nicholas nor Madame Natalia were looking at her. She added: 'You weren't exactly tactful about it.'

'As I recall, you asked us to be blunt.'

'So I did. I'm sorry. This has . . . upset me as much as it has you.'

'Not *quite* as much, perhaps.' Nicholas was regaining his old acidity. It made her smile. 'Well, no, perhaps not quite as much.' She looked at Abbott who had stayed in the room because he was an interested party, but deferentially and in an attentive position near the drinks because he was also a servant. 'Abbott, I shall leave the hotel tomorrow morning. I wonder if I could sleep in the small room I had when I stayed here all those years ago?'

'There are very much nicer guest suites.'

'I know, but I'd like that one.'

'Very good, Madam.'

There was not much more to be said there and then, though a very great deal to be said elsewhere and later. The gathering broke up. Natalia Beaumont asked Nicholas to lunch, doubtless in order to discuss, before her son rejoined his unit, where they all stood and what should be done about it. Madame Lavallier faded away to her own living-quarters in one of the further buildings surrounding the courtyard. David Rudd was returning to the coast where he elected to stay; he would return tomorrow morning and they would then 'get down to business'. Monsieur Gosselin drove Catherine back to the hotel. Abbott was left to clear away their empty glasses — thoughtfully.

The reading of Edward Walden's will was over.

PART THREE

To him that will, ways are not wanting.
GEORGE HERBERT

CHAPTER 1

Madame Albert, patronne of the Hôtel de la Poste, patted her curls—far too red this week, that stupid hairdresser!—and said, 'So Mademoiselle is now in residence.'

'At the château?'

'You mean you hadn't heard?'

Madame Bonnet eyed the disastrous coiffure with secret glee. She, however, had no one but herself to blame for the fact that her large nose was raw and peeling; she'd fallen asleep in the sun once too often. 'When?'

'Paid her bill and left the day before yesterday.'

'And Le Grand Monsieur?' Their private name for Nicholas Tate referred to the notorious brother of Louis XIV who, as every French schoolchild knows, had shared Mr Tate's sexual proclivities.

'Departed. No prize for guessing where he's staying now.'

'At Natalia Beaumont's, of course.'

'Of course.'

'So we infer,' said the pharmacist's wife, picking at dried skin delicately, 'that everything really *was* left to the girl.'

'I hear nothing definite.'

'Doctor Sarazin was actually there, you know.'

'At the reading of the will?' Madame Albert's turn to be surprised. How had she missed hearing this? Could it be that certain of her informants no longer trusted her? 'In expectation of some legacy, no doubt. He looked after Monsieur Edouard for many years.'

'Such an irritating man. He's in and out of the pharmacy all day, but he never talks, not even to my

husband.' Doctor Sarazin componded this infamy by
being a widower, no attentive wife to share his troubles
and publicize his secrets. Madame Bonnet showed her
horse-teeth in a smile. 'If it really all went to her, what a
smack in the eye for the others!'

'If I know the others,' replied the patronne, and she
did, 'it won't rest there.'

'Julie Gosselin came in for some sleeping-pills — she
takes far too many, by the way.'

'So would I, with Paul for a husband!'

'She says that mistresses and illegitimate children have
to be *specifically* named in a will, or they have no rights at
all, not legally.'

'She's probably got it wrong, you know how silly she is!'

'I don't think so, she seemed quite certain. Paul is
looking after the daughter's interests.'

'Not alone, I trust. He's a hopeless lawyer.'

'I understand the English one's still here.'

Madame Albert sniffed. 'Oh, him!' But the whole town
knew that her attitude to David Rudd was a matter of
sour grapes, because in all his visits to Montferrat he had
never once stayed at her hotel when there was no room for
him at La Bastide, preferring some tourist trap down on
the coast.

Thinking of Englishmen, Madame Bonnet said, 'I
suppose the manservant's come out of it all right, they
always do.'

'Naturally. They know too much.'

'What do you suppose will happen to him?'

'At the moment he's still there.' The patronne was not
interested in Abbott, who had proved many years before
that he was not a source of information; snubbed her in
the process too! 'The girl would be a fool to keep him on,
but then I don't suppose that will enter into it, she's
bound to sell the place.'

'If it's hers to sell.'

'I think we can assume it is. Don't pick at your nose, dear, you're making it worse! As long as the others don't find a way of doing her out of it.'

'Julie says that's impossible too. I wonder what Marianne Lavallier thinks about it all.'

'Well, we know that she doesn't think very much,' said Madame Albert, again patting the disastrous curls, 'God not having given her very much to think with! But as usual her good-for-nothing son was a bit quicker on the uptake — *now* we see why he was chasing the girl.'

'He can't do much, she's his half-sister.'

'Since when has that deterred the local peasantry?'

'*She's* hardly a peasant!'

'No, but if she's anything like her father she's not very particular — remember the water-ski instructor?'

Madame Bonnet showed all her awesome teeth in a girlish laugh. 'And that creature from the night-club in Cannes!'

'A sword-swallower, wasn't she?'

This particular innuendo always had her friend rolling in the aisle. 'Ernestine, you are *terrible*, she was a dancer.' The laughter faded abruptly. 'Oh!'

'What's the matter?'

'If the girl *has* been left the château, and if she sells it . . .'

'What?'

'Don't you see?'

'I see she'll have a difficult time finding a buyer for a place that size. Nobody wants an expensive hotel stuck right out here, but I suppose it might make a nice monastery . . .'

'If she sells it,' wailed Madame Bonnet, 'We'll have nothing to talk about, ever again.'

The patronne smiled. 'But in the meantime, dear, the situation is positively *explosive* — I do so hope no one gets hurt when it blows up.'

CHAPTER 2

David Rudd and Paul Gosselin were constantly surprised by Catherine's grasp of finance and property. Giving her his most charming smile, Mr Rudd would say, 'Ah, I can see you're your father's daughter!' To which Catherine would reply, 'I worked in advertising for three years. I do know what money means, how it's used.'

When, weightily, Monsieur Gosselin began to explain the intricacies of moving large sums of money out of France, she said, 'But why move it?'

'Then you intend to be resident here?'

'Surely it doesn't matter where I'm resident—there's nothing to stop me taking a flat in Paris and *establishing* residence. Is there?' And so on.

Her proposals for an arrangement to take care of Natalia Beaumont, Marianne Lavallier and Nicholas Tate were generous. Over-generous in David Rudd's opinion, but Catherine was adamant: 'You both knew my father better than I did, and I suppose you were fond of him—you keep saying how good or nice he was about this or that. But I think he must have been vain and selfish and . . . yes, cruel. If they'd been right, if I *had* been cut out completely, it wouldn't have surprised me in the least. I'd have been disappointed and hurt, but not surprised. And now . . . Don't you see? I'm not being generous at all, I'm only trying to be fair.'

What, they both wondered, was this cool child actually feeling?

Among other things, Catherine was feeling as if prison gates had opened to reveal a sunny and beautiful landscape beyond the dark walls. Always a slow waker in the mornings, she would become aware of a vague feeling of comfortable expectation long before her drowsy brain knew the exact reason for it. Then she would open her eyes and look at the relatively small and unimportant room where she had chosen to sleep, and the whole new world she had inherited would gradually take possession of her senses, enfolding her in a warm security such as she had never known before, not even in childhood.

Her reason for choosing this particular suite was not fanciful, nor had she any wish to create an effect, as Abbott, she was sure, suspected. No, a great many things had to be exorcized, not the least important, and importunate, being that unhappy thirteen-year-old who had once slept in this bed for three uncertain weeks, trapped in the awkwardness of puberty and an incoherent upbringing. She had not yet gone away, that plump little ghost, but she was beginning to recede.

Opening the bedroom shutters on the translucent Mediterranean mornings, if she awoke before Isabelle called her with a jug of orange-juice at eight o'clock, Catherine could now look out on the world without uncertainty, and with only minor fears hardly worth bothering about, in the knowledge that it was hers to explore and enjoy. The long prison sentence was over. She was free.

On this particular morning, however, the moment of simple pleasure was marred by the only sight capable of denting her gratification; the opening shutters revealed Pascal among the vines, walking slowly away from her with Latouche, the factor, one of those hitherto unseen persons whose labours upheld the easy life of 'le château'. She watched the younger man bend to examine a vine and straighten up, gesticulating. He looked so jaunty and carefree out there in the early sunshine that she, in her bedroom, experienced an obscure and uncomfortable sensation of still being trapped. The thought crossed her mind that he was truly at liberty, within himself, as she could never be. She dismissed it impatiently; they were entirely dissimilar people in every way, so how could the degree of their individual freedoms be compared?

Apart from this, the fact remained that those broad shoulders, that strong and suntanned neck, gleaming black hair, easy-going swagger, were a continuing irritation, the only irritation in her bright new world. She remembered the uninhibited ardour of their embrace in a tangle of bougainvillæa; knew that she would always remember it because it had been a sensual counterpart of her moment of triumph. The sooner she could conclude her business here, and escape from this lusty and desirable young man, the better. After all, the world was full of lusty and desirable young men, none of whom were likely to turn out to be her half-brother!

She put on a housecoat and went downstairs to breakfast, passing on the way a Renoir, several watercolour sketches by Constable and, at the foot of the stairs, Rembrandt's old lady. She must remember that the man from Sotheby-Parke Bernet was arriving tomorrow, and the man from the Metropolitan Museum in New York the day after. If the man from the Rijksmuseum chose to come on the same day, so much the better: Amsterdam and New York could escalate each other's bids: unless she agreed to David Rudd's crafty plan of *giving* the picture to the Louvre in exchange for enormous and valuable tax exemptions.

How interesting it all was, profits aside! So much more interesting than a typewriter on Madison Avenue, the lunch-time salad at a noisy Automat, the fending off of junior executives in the elevator. Of course she ought to be sending postcards to her friends in New York, they would all be wondering how she was enjoying her 'vacation', but there seemed little point when she would never be seeing any of them ever again. Life with Mother, and without Mother, had taught Catherine Walden to be a realist.

Partly in order to change established precedents, and partly because she preferred to look down the wide valley rather than at an enclosed garden, she had taken to having her breakfast on the circular terrace at the foot of the tower. Here, in an angle created by a massive buttress, and not far away from the historical bougainvillæa, sunshades composed a secluded oasis; there was invariably a gentle breeze.

Abbott, appearing with the coffee, said, 'Good morning, Madam, a beautiful morning.' And later, presenting the croissants, 'I'm having a little trouble with a tooth, Madam, I wonder if I might take an hour or two off this afternoon to visit the dentist.' It was another of his small private jokes to present this chestnut of an excuse when he could so easily have invented something more subtle.

'The dentist' was Madame Natalia Beaumont who had convened a meeting at her smart little house in the hills above Montferrat. She and Nicholas, both experienced in business and therefore knowing something about litigation, had realized that before any legal steps could be taken they must all consolidate their reasons for believing that Edward Walden had ever intended to make a second will; they must also find, if possible, some shred of concrete evidence that he had actually done so. The inclusion of Pascal at any such meeting was debatable, and they had debated at length. His fiendish laughter had not been forgotten, and might never be forgiven, but on the other hand he stood to lose as much as anyone else, and if he wasn't asked to attend, Marianne would be hurt.

As for Abbott, while it was true that neither of them liked or trusted him, there was no denying that in certain respects he had been closer to his master than had any of the master's bedfellows, and for much longer; therefore his presence was vital, he was a prime source of information.

'Of course,' said Natalia, 'we must be careful what we say in front of him.'

Nicholas agreed, but he had an idea that once they'd all got the bit between their teeth, prudence would be cast aside and everybody would say exactly what came into their heads. Not that this mattered, because Abbott probably knew more than they did anyway.

Jean-Michel had returned to his unit at Besançon. Neither his mother nor Nicholas mentioned the absence because they both knew that any meeting could well do without his particular brand of muddle-headed, quasi-heroic defiance. Besides, he and Pascal might once again come to blows, and if they could break china in the large library at La Bastide there was nothing to stop them wrecking the whole of Natalia's pretty little sitting-room and everything in it.

The Lavalliers arrived, Marianne squeezed into an unfortunate blue and white dress which Nicholas associated exclusively with a certain kind of British actress appearing in a certain kind of West End comedy. Her son, determinedly sardonic, wore tight jeans and a T-shirt, in sharp contrast to Abbott who presently appeared in a natty pale grey suit of impeccable cut, which made Nicholas wonder, as everybody had always wondered, about his very private private-life: what on earth did he get up to, where and who with?

Madame Beaumont opened the proceedings. 'I thought we ought to meet before I see my lawyer. He's going to ask me what reason we all have for believing that Edward made a second will in which we were . . . remembered.'

Marianne Lavallier felt awkward in this graceful room.

She was swinging her foot up and down, staring at it as though it didn't belong to her, but her willingness to speak at once seemed to indicate that she had prepared her piece and wanted to get it off her chest. Still gazing at her shoe, she said, 'He . . . We discussed it at the very beginning. All right . . .' She looked up at them with a trace of defiance. 'It was different for me, I was the housekeeper, I wasn't smart and clever, I didn't belong to . . . all that. I told him so when we . . . became lovers, I said it wasn't going to change me, I was born a servant and I'd stay a servant . . .'

Pascal said, 'Pah!' His mother's eyes flashed. 'Give yourself airs if you like, it's what I was. In a way it's why he liked me. There! That's said.' She squared her shoulders. 'So then . . . Well, you may think it sounds — what's the word? — mercenary, but it wasn't. It wasn't, because we weren't equals. We talked about money — he told me that I'd never have to go without, he'd look after me. And later, when I had his son, he said it again — I'd be taken care of. He said it a dozen times. And you?'

Neither her tone of voice, nor the stare which she directed at Madame Beaumont were friendly, but the latter was too clever to worry about such things at this particular moment. With any luck they'd never again have to sit together in the same room, so that anything which needed to be said, antagonistic or not, had better be said now.

'With me it wasn't so different. Our relationship went further back, lasted longer, but . . .' She shook her head. 'Nobody stays "in love" forever. When it was over . . . We all know that he needed me around — substitute wife, hostess, call it what you like. And it was the same with me — after I'd had Jean-Michel he told me that the child would be taken care of, it was always understood.' She made an impatient gesture. 'Of *course* it was understood, he mentioned it a hundred times over the years. He was very generous with presents and so on, both you and Pascal know that too, but when he said "taken care of" he can only have meant after his death, in his will.' She spread her beautiful hands and looked at Nicholas.

'I think we're asking the wrong question. We needn't doubt that he intended to leave us money, that's obvious. But what did he say about *not* leaving anything to his wife? A good deal, as far as I'm concerned.'

'Oh yes, and to me.' Madame Lavallier obviously felt herself to be on firmer ground here. 'He hated her. He blamed her for their son's death, he said it was all her fault that the marriage broke up.'

'Also,' said Nicholas, 'he didn't take to his daughter at all, that time she came to stay.'

'Poor child!'

'Okay, Natalia, poor child! but we're looking for the truth—and the truth is he detested Laura and disliked their daughter. Is it conceivable that he should have left them everything?'

'Not conceivable that he *meant* to leave them everything, no.'

'So let's see *when* he might have made a second will. I saw him in October last year, and he hadn't made it then because—I can remember his actual words—he said, "I really must pull myself together and do something about all of you, the people who mean most to me." When did David Rudd last visit him?'

Abbott said, 'A month after you, November.'

'And that's when he said, "Don't bully me, David, I'm thinking about it.' So if he *did* make a will it was after that, with some other lawyer, and I don't mean Paul Gosselin because he'd have mentioned it long ago.'

'I think not, sir.' Because Abbott had kept silent for so long his utterances had a corresponding weight. 'Mr Edward was quite weak by then, unable to leave the house. Correct, Madame?'

Natalia Beaumont nodded.

'If anyone came to see him I knew about it. They didn't, not any strangers, not after November.'

'And,' said Marianne, 'there'd have been witnesses, a will has to be witnessed.'

'Anyone at La Bastide could have done that.' Nicholas was not about to give up so easily. 'The manager, what's his name . . . ?'

'Latouche,' said Abbott inexorably, 'would have been mentioned in a later will, he was there when Mr Edward bought the place. In fact the entire staff would have received something, however small. And interested parties are not legally allowed to witness a will, I think I'm correct.'

He was. Nicholas leaned back in his chair, biting a fingernail. With a touch of desperation, Natalia Beaumont said, 'But, Abbott, you surely think he *made* a second will?'

The faded eyes met hers steadily, sign, it's said, of an expert liar. 'No, Madame, I don't. I think he intended to, but like many another sick man he left it too late.' The words fell like heavy stones upon the frail craft of their expectancy, weighing it down, sinking it.

'Also,' said Abbott, 'if I may say so without offence —' an invariable sign that he was about to give it — 'Mademoiselle Catherine has been extremely generous as far as I'm concerned. I doubt if Mr Edward would have done more, and I understand she's made similar arrangements for all of you.'

'That,' replied Madame Beaumont firmly, 'is neither here nor there. We're grateful, of course, but . . .' She hesitated to voice the cliché, and was reasonably sure that, given time, Marianne Lavallier would do it for her.

Marianne obliged. 'It's the principle of the thing, isn't it?'

Nicholas and Natalia agreed politely. Abbott was silent.

Pascal said, 'You haven't asked me what *I* think, but then you never do. I think the money was his, nothing to do with us. If he'd chosen to give it all to the Church or throw it into the sea, that was his business. As a matter of fact, he said a lot of things about it to me, he even offered to send me to college, but I told him I wasn't clever enough, it would only be a waste — I said I'd rather have a really good, fast car, so he bought me the Mercedes. He talked about his will too . . .'

A distinct quickening of interest greeted this.

'He told me I'd get a lot of money from it, but I didn't pay much attention — he used to say things like that to . . . you know, keep you on a string. That's why he liked me, he knew he wasn't fooling me the way he kept fooling you — at least I suppose he did, or you wouldn't be sitting here now, talking a lot of hot air . . .'

'Pascal!'

'Oh, for God's sake, Mother, let me speak. The fact is, he kept us all for years and we all had a marvellous time at his expense, and anyone who didn't save a bit while the going was good ought to have their head examined. No use crying over spilt milk, it's done, we're on our own.'

'Pascal, that's enough!'

'It's always enough every time I open my mouth. I don't see why Mademoiselle Catherine shouldn't have it, she's got more right to it than any of us.'

'Which is probably why,' suggested Nicholas acidly, 'you made a pass or two at her.'

If he imagined that this would disconcert Pascal he was wrong; all he got by way of answer was a wicked grin.

Marianne was saying, 'Why do I have to keep apologizing for you? Why can't you ever behave properly? We'd better be going.'

'For God's sake, yes — the whole thing's stupid anyway.'

Natalia Beaumont was unruffled by this farouche performance: 'But, Pascal, you stand to lose as much as we do.'

He shrugged.

'And money *is* important, particularly to a young man. You could buy your own land, your own vineyard.' She knew exactly what she was doing; there isn't a peasant in the world upon whom the magic word 'land' doesn't exert its pull.

He shrugged again, but less dismissively. She continued: 'And another thing—because you have a . . . special relationship with Mademoiselle Catherine you're likely to hear more than we are, about what's going on . . .'

'You want me to spy on her.'

'I didn't say that, and for all I know you're not interested in having your own land.' The word could not be repeated too often. 'Land doesn't mean as much to your generation as it once did, which is probably a good thing. But whatever you imagine you think, Pascal, your interests lie with us, not with her.'

Having gone this far, it seemed to her that nothing could be lost by continuing to the end: 'After all, you can't marry her, if that's at the back of your mind, she's your half-sister.'

He raised his dark eyes and looked at her directly. 'Pity, she'd have me tomorrow. And then,' he added wickedly, 'I'd own plenty of the land you seem to think I'm so stuck on. Wouldn't I?'

Madame Beaumont smiled back. 'Obviously you'll do as you think fit. She could well say things to you she wouldn't dream of saying to anyone else.'

Pascal shook his head, but Madame Natalia, catching his mother's eye, was sure that she could now rely on some direct information. Mothers often know what their sons are thinking before they know it themselves. In the case of her own Jean-Michel, she had periodically wished that this wasn't the case.

When they'd all gone, Nicholas said, 'We didn't get very far, did we?'

'Oh I don't know. The air's a little clearer, we all know where we stand.'

'I'm not sure that I know where Pascal stands.'

'With us.' She smiled. 'He's not that woman's son for nothing.'

'And Abbott?'

'Yes, Abbott.' The smile faded. She began to pace about her pretty room. 'He's up to something.'

'What makes you think so?'

'I was watching him. He changed, suddenly, right in the middle of a sentence. Something struck him, something we missed.' She came to a pause, looking out over the town and the shimmering hills beyond. 'Yes, Abbott's up to something!'

CHAPTER 3

Though it was self-evidently impossible for any of Sotheby's employees to show actual enthusiasm, their Mr Courtenay-James, a languid gentleman in his late thirties with a strangulated Oxbridge voice, was having to make visible efforts to present a correct façade to the seller, in this case Catherine. 'Yes indeed, that's a very . . . that's a rather distinguished piece;' and, 'To be frank, I've never . . . seldom seen anything of that age in such perfect, or should one say near-perfect, condition,' and even, with a slight start, '*Oh!*'

'What's the matter, Mr Courtenay-James?'

'One had always understood . . .' A closer look. 'I must

say I thought this was in the Victoria and Albert. One, ah —' nervous laugh — 'lives and learns.'

Nicholas's annotated catalogue, which he had left behind for Catherine's convenience, kept Mr Courtenay-James quiet for a long time; then, 'A slight *over*-valuation here and there, perhaps. Dear me, I hadn't realized that there were *two* Renoirs.'

Presently he became much more thoughtful, and finally said, 'Our Mr Price and Charles Willoughby-Scott will have to be called in. I wasn't told . . . Of course one realized that it was a very *special* collection, but . . .' Final collapse. 'A great deal of this is right outside my field, I'm primarily porcelain, you see.'

Primarily Porcelain had barely retired to the study to make some telephone calls when Abbott announced, 'Mr Schreiber, the gentleman who called from the airport, is in the library, Madam.'

Mr Schreiber was from the Metropolitan Museum of Art in New York. Though he apologized earnestly for arriving a day earlier than expected, he was obviously delighted to reach La Bastide before his colleague from the Getty Museum in Santa Monica, not to mention others from every other part of the world.

As it happened, Dr Hans Vanleyden from the Rijksmuseum also chanced to arrive a day early, while Mr Schreiber was actually examining the Rembrandt. Exquisite courtesy ensued. Primarily Porcelain, emerging from the study with all manner of cartes blanches from Sotheby-Parke Bernet, was horrified to find himself in such illustrious and affluent company, and doubled back to the telephone post-haste to turn financial screws.

Catherine thought it wise to retire with Monsieur Gosselin and David Rudd to the sanctuary of her terrace overlooking the valley, hidden from view by the bulk of the tower, for the house itself was beginning to thrum with the professional rivalry contained inside it.

Mr Rudd had heard from England that his wife's condition, following the operation, was improving; this news, coupled with first reactions from the artistic world, put them all in good humour, and they made plans with enthusiasm. Rudd was going to leave for Paris and London as soon as he had settled matters with Madame Lavallier's lawyer in Toulon and Madame Beaumont's lawyer in Marseille; then, having discussed matters with the French tax authorities and having drawn up a full list of Edward Walden's assets, he would return to Montferrat bearing the many documents requiring Catherine's signature.

In the meantime, Monsieur Gosselin would keep an eye on the art experts and begin the doubtless lengthy procedure of selling La Bastide, the vineyard, the farms, the spreading hectares of arable land and olive groves.

Once the major museums had made their bids for the more outstanding objects in the collection, the remainder would be sent to auction. Even the most rough and ready assessment of what all this would return in cash, after tax, sent the mind reeling. Though Catherine had grown used to the idea that she was going to be a very rich woman, she was quite unable to assimilate the amount of money involved. The two lawyers, in spite of professional reticence, made no effort to hide their satisfaction. Monsieur Gosselin went so far as to call the prospect 'highly edifying', while Mr Rudd went further: 'I've a feeling that quite a few records are going to be broken in the next few days.'

It was perhaps ironical that Abbott was at that very moment interesting himself in records of a rather different, and seemingly more mundane, nature.

At the end of the long gallery and up a worn flight of stone steps was a room known as The Office. This was the lair of a certain Mademoiselle Foch, one of those dedicated and scrawny spinster secretaries, often sporting a faint moustache, who are well-known in every place of business throughout the world.

Her mother having died suddenly, she had found herself in possession of a small villa at Montferrat and an income to go with it; she had also, very quickly, found herself bored. A neatly-typed notice in the window of the Tabac had led her, to her surprise, into the presence of the legendary and notorious Edward Walden. She was exactly what he wanted; her face ensured that she would never marry and desert him, while her scorn for every last female inhabitant of Montferrat ensured that she would never gossip about his private affairs.

Mademoiselle Foch imagined that she and her employer were the only people in possession of keys to The Office, but naturally Abbott also had a set. He let himself into the fusty little room, smelling of Mademoiselle Foch's insipid cologne and old papers which tend to yellow and crumble quickly in the climate of the Var.

Using another key, Abbott unlocked a filing cabinet and looked swiftly through the alphabetical sections. Yes, here it was: Builders and Decorators, a massive collection of estimates and bills covering the past five years. After half a decade at Mademoiselle Foch's fingertips, old bills were relegated to a store-cupboard in the corner where they could moulder peacefully, disturbed only by mice.

Abbott's fingers came to rest near the end of the section; searched to and fro; drew out a particular account: 'Pierre Corrado et Cie, 3 rue Athénée, Toulon. La Bastide de Peyrol. To replacing two windows, first floor, south face—Repairing four windows, first floor, north face. To re-flooring four square metres in Long Gallery, damaged by dry-rot. To redecorating overall where necessary: one coat primer, one undercoat, three coats . . .'

Abbott nodded to himself. This was it all right. He

made a note of the invoice number and the date; then replaced the bill in its proper slot — Mademoiselle Foch always noticed the slightest alteration in her meticulous arrangements — closed the filing cabinet, locked it, let herself out into the passage, locked the door of The Office, and went downstairs to supervise the preparation of luncheon. He was well pleased with himself.

After the meal, and to escape from the art experts who were now engaged in preliminary skirmishing without having yet made a formal declaration of war, Catherine went back to the terrace and lay down in a hammock. Shade was creeping around the tower and a gentle breeze blew off the valley so that even here, high above the olive trees, she was lulled by the susurration of their leaves. She closed her eyes; dozed off perhaps; then was suddenly aware of not being alone. Pascal stood looking down at her.

The British side of her character would like to have said, 'Pascal, La Bastide is my house, and you are the son of the housekeeper, please keep to your own quarters,' but American Catherine could say nothing so undemocratic. The social conundrum was further complicated by the sexual one: she was by no means averse to his presence though she would have preferred to be unaffected by it.

'You even look nice when you're asleep. Most people look awful and sloppy.'

'I saw you out in the vineyard this morning.'

'Latouche says it's going to be a wonderful year. I hope you don't sell before the vendange.'

'Sometimes, when its as beautiful as this, I don't want to sell at all.'

'Mother says you're making a . . . very generous arrangement for us. Thank you.' She examined his face for irony but found none. Meeting her eyes, he added,

'Madame Beaumont held a little council of war yesterday.'

'Did she?'

'Mother, Abbott, Nicky Tate, me.'

'And?'

'Oh, nothing really, nothing we didn't all know before.. They won't give up, you know.'

The grey eyes grew sharper, the examination more concentrated. Then she nodded. 'I see.'

'What do you see?'

'You've been instructed to make me feel . . . uneasy, guilty.'

'In fact,' he replied, at his most frank and charming, 'I was instructed to spy on you and report back.'

'And is that what you're doing?'

'Does it sound like it?'

She shook her head, half-smiling. 'I'm not a fool, Pascal, don't treat me like one.'

'Meaning?'

'Meaning, dear half-brother, that double games are your second nature, you told me so.'

He nodded. 'Yes, I like double games.'

'You can report that I don't feel in the least uneasy or guilty. I've got the law behind me.'

He put his head on one side and considered this, black eyes alight with mischief. 'It might be more fun to tell them you're suffering agonies of remorse. Or—' he laughed, slapping his thigh, looking at that moment like any young peasant anywhere along the littoral from Malaga to the islands of Greece—'or I could tell them that you're furious with them for sending me to spy, and you've changed your mind, you aren't giving them a penny after all!'

She had to smile, but she said, 'One of these days you'll trip over your own cleverness, maybe break your neck.'

'So my mother tells me three or four times a week.

They're right about one thing, all the same.'
'What?'
'He certainly meant to make that second will.'
'How do we know? All we know is that he didn't.'
'I wonder if you'd have been in it. They think not, of course.'
'They told me that in no uncertain terms.' She closed her eyes, wishing he would go away, but to the contrary he sat down on one of the chairs and lay back. 'The house is full of schoolmasters.'
'They're art experts, but I know what you mean.'
'Are you really selling everything?'
She cocked an eye at him. 'Do they want to know that too?'
'Oh come *on*, I'm just talking.'
'If you wanted to "just talk" to me you shouldn't have told me about Madame's meeting, and them wanting you to get information out of me.'
'But the very fact I told you proves I'm not doing anything of the sort.'
There was no reply. She had closed her eyes again.
'Well, doesn't it?'
'No, Pascal, it doesn't.'
Her cool rejection suddenly angered him. He stood up again abruptly. 'You don't honestly think I'd spy on *you*—for *them?*'
'I wouldn't put it beyond you.'
'Then you don't understand the first thing about me.'
She opened her eyes and gave the anger a judicious glance. 'Perhaps I understand too much.'
'Now you're being stupid.'
'*I'm* being stupid! You want everything your own way, don't you? You think you can lie to people *and* have them trust you—well, that's not how it goes.'
'Oh, I see! Now you're playing the grand châtelaine, owner of La Bastide.'

'I'm not "playing" anything, I *am* the owner of La Bastide, I'd like to go to sleep, and you're boring me.' She turned her back on hime. He stared at it in mute fury.

Marianne Lavallier was watching this tableau from an upstairs window. She turned away from it, and stood for a few seconds in thought; then went to the linen-room and collected some of the best towels. Thus armed, she walked down the corridor, turned right into a lesser one, and stopped in front of a door. She half expected it to be locked; in the old days, bedroom doors at La Bastide had been locked at all times of day, for a variety of different reasons; but it wasn't. She entered the unpretentious suite where Catherine had elected to sleep.

Keeping the towels over her arm, just in case, she began to search drawers and cupboards. She wasn't looking for anything in particular, and the search had nothing to do with Natalia Beaumont and her meeting of conspirators: at least only in so far as this had provided an additional purpose for the investigation. The fact was that she liked examining other people's possessions and had always done so, more out of good old country curiosity than for any more devious reason.

She had first formed the habit after Monsieur Edouard had concluded his swift winter courtship and conducted her to his bed. Only then was she overcome by an urge to know more about the mysterious and unknowable lives which were entwined with that of her lover. After a little practice she was able to form a very exact picture of the people concerned.

Take Mademoiselle Catherine. Here was a girl with an orderly mind; not rich, for some of her clothing was little more than serviceable, but possessing several very good things. Americans, Marianne had learned, could buy dressy and expensive-looking garments quite cheaply — one had to examine the seams in order to discover the hasty mechanical workmanship which betrayed them. She had a few nice pieces of jewellery — no shoddy imitations; that showed taste and a dislike of false show.

She had left home for a short stay abroad, so there wasn't a lot of clothing: all rather quiet, dull in Marianne's opinion, but experience had taught her that this often indicated good family, even extreme wealth, so she tended to be wary in her sartorial judgements.

Of course the girl was on the pill, but the female guests always were: including far too many Catholics (Marianne was conventional in her faith). Her perfumes were Calèche and, for more dressy occasions, Cabochard, old-fashioned for a young girl, but good.

Like almost everyone else, Catherine had put the folder containing her passport, tickets, traveller's cheques and so on, in the top right-hand drawer of the chest, under some underwear. Owing to her romantic ideas concerning travel and the lure of foreign places, Marianne always derived particular enjoyment from examination of these harmless documents. And had not Mademoiselle come flying in from New York itself, city of unimaginable towers? One day when Marianne had received her share, large or small, of Monsieur Edouard's estate she too would sit in a huge aeroplane, leaving France for the first time; she might even go to New York, stand on top of the tallest tower.

Was it this miraculous thought, or another, which made her pause. Catherine's travel-folder in one hand, gazing out of the window at the vineyard, lost in meditation?

Pascal was still angry, and the fact that Catherine, after turning her back, had indeed fallen into a deep sleep made him angrier still. He trailed across the somnolent garden; he kicked at stones; he kicked at the base of a statue which he particularly disliked, hurting his toe in the process. For a few moments he stood and listened to droning voices from inside the house: '. . . and our government is very aware of the fact that although he was a Dutchman we actually possess a disproportionately small number of his major works . . .'

Pascal glared at the placid surface of the pool; he would have liked to shatter it by jumping in, but lacked the energy. Instead, he walked through several of the smaller basins in the Italian garden and then sploshed into his mother's little house, discarding the wet shoes in her kitchen.

At the top of the stairs was a door leading to the main part of La Bastide. Madame Lavallier had left this open, which was why her son, on reaching the top step, was just in time to see her coming out of the room occupied by Catherine. He knew it well because a couple of times, at night, he had tried the door (you never knew your luck) and found it locked.

When Marianne saw him she betrayed slight confusion which nobody but this son, so close to her, would have been able to identify.

'Hello!' he said, 'Snooping again?' For she had once, over a third glass of cognac, confessed the habit.

'No, just putting some fresh towels.'

Pascal's anger was receding; he looked at her with irritated affection. Her inattention to detail as far as lies were concerned always amused him; any mother of his ought to know better! If she had really been changing towels the ones over her arm would be dirty, instead of being so obviously clean, fresh frm the linen-room.

The ironic amusement made her flush. 'As if I would!'

'Find anything interesting?'

She snorted and turned away. He went into his room and flung himself on the bed, staring at the woolly rabbit, Catherine's Hoopla prize, which she had given to him on that complicated night from which so many further complications had since developed. Oh, to hell with her! La grande châtelaine, he'd very soon find a way of taking *her* down a peg or two. Presently he dozed off.

One of the windows of the bedroom overlooked the stableyard, most of the stalls now converted into garages with staff quarters above them. Thus Pascal, who was never so deep in sleep that he wasn't aware of the slightest unaccustomed sound, was aware of Abbott starting the motor of his little Peugeot. The young man wondered vaguely where he might be going on such a hot afternoon but was not unduly interested and very quickly fell into deeper sleep.

The next sound which impinged on his consciousness, again that of a car being started up, was a different matter altogether, for he recognized it as the Range-Rover which only he and the chauffeur, Daniel, were permitted to drive, apart from the late Edward Walden, naturally. Daniel had gone to Paris to see his family, and in any case nobody but Pascal's own mother could possibly make such a hash of those gears.

He slipped off his bed and went to the window. Yes, there she was, wearing her best blue and white, red in the face from exertion; she had no feel for a car whatsoever, and had on more than one occasion been requested not to use the Range-Rover. Crash-clunk! The engine stalled. She restarted it impatiently; then drove in a haphazard manner out of the gate. This, with the front door, was the only entrance to La Bastide, so that the ancient building was still, to all intents and purposes, the fortress intended by its original builders.

Where was she going, all on her own? She detested driving, always asked him to drive her. And why the best dress? Not difficult questions to answer. Pascal went back to sleep.

To say that Madame Lavallier drove straight to Madame

Beaumont's house would not be correct, though this was indeed her intention. For a start, like Catherine on another occasion, she found herself trapped behind the local bus, and followed it without thinking so that she ended up in the centre of Montferrat instead of on the leafy road leading into the hills above the town. She then became confused by the one-way system which must certainly have been changed since she had last ventured out in a car by herself; however, by the simple expedient of driving down one of the streets in the wrong direction, narrowly avoiding collision with Monsieur Fouquet's van driven by that stupid younger son, she soon corrected her error.

Apart from nearly smashing her way through the wall which edged Madame Beaumont's drive—how inconvenient they were, these hillside villas!—she arrived without further incident, hot and exasperated, and her best blue and white a shade crumpled; she really must lose weight.

Natalia Beaumont and Nicholas Tate, both a little pale from having witnessed her encounter with the wall, protection from a fifty-foot drop, were waiting expectantly. Marianne was settled into a comfortable chair on the terrace and given a citron pressé.

The urgency of the telephone call which had alerted them to her imminent arrival seemed to have given way to a disinclination for speech, but Madame Beaumont knew her guest well and said bluntly, 'So, my dear, what is this important thing you've discovered?'

'I . . . I happened to be . . . replacing some items of underwear which I'd washed for Mademoiselle—in her chest of drawers . . .'

Natalia and Nicholas Tate, both of whom knew all about the habitual examination of any guest's possessions, avoided each other's eye.

'And?'

'Well, I just happened to see one of those travel-folder things, you know what I mean?'

'Yes.'

'Well . . .'

It was not the first time that Abbott had visited the establishment of Pierre Corrado et Cie, builders and decorators, of the rue Athénée in Toulon, having had occasion to complain more than once when the quality of their work had not satisfied Edward Walden. He was received by Corrado père in person, an honour accorded to few.

Abbott had dressed with his usual care, a fawn suit with a slight check today, and before leaving La Bastide he had instructed the maid on duty, Isabelle, regarding her afternoon functions: tea in the library for the artistic gentlemen, tea in the shade of the tower for Madame: so that he now felt able to relax and to take things slowly which, in the Var, particularly when dealing with the older generation, was essential.

He accepted Monsieur Corrado's expressions of sorrow at his master's death, evaded his discreet enquiries as to the contents of the will and the ultimate fate of La Bastide, and eventually arrived at the point of his visit. 'You remember,' he said in his dreadful but colloquial French, 'the work you did last November, repairing some windows and a piece of flooring with dry rot in it?'

Monsieur Corrado didn't remember exactly, so Abbott gave him the invoice number; they examined the estimate together.

'The work was not to Monsieur Walden's liking?'

'No, no—he said he thought it had been excellently carried out. I'm afraid I'm the one at fault. I was rather inattentive at the time, Mr Walden being so ill, and I forgot to make a note of something one of your men told me: to do with the position of hot water pipes under the floor. We don't want to tear the whole thing up.'

'If there's trouble with the plumbing I can easily send one of my . . .'

'No trouble at all. I'm thinking of the future. If, for instance, the house is sold — one likes these things to be in order.'

'Ah.'

'I'm sure the man would remember, he was very helpful at the time; if I could ask him which side of the gallery those pipes are on and which bedrooms they serve, you understand me?'

Monsieur Corrado Senior thought that it was a somewhat finicky question, particularly since Monsieur Walden was now dead, but on the other hand this manservant would doubtless go to a new post with an equally rich employer, and might, if properly handled, bring a lot more business to Corrado and Company; so he said that he understood completely and could very soon ascertain which of his men had worked on the new floor. Abbott was pleased; graciously accepted a glass of pastis while underlings carried out the necessary research.

The results were not so pleasing. One of the men, the elderly one, had fallen off some scaffolding only six weeks after the work at La Bastide had been completed: no surprise to Abbott who was constantly amazed by the average French workman's daily intake of rough red wine. Fractured ribs had pierced his lung; he had died just before Christmas of a pulmonary complication. The younger man, Jules Perrault, had left Monsieur Corrado's employ to set up his own business in Nice. Which of the two had spoken so helpfully to Abbott?

'The young one.' Obviously, since the other was in no position to answer his questions.

'Then we will telephone at once. I have the number.'

Abbott assured him that this wasn't necessary; as it happened he was going into Nice on his next day off and would call upon Jules Perrault himself. Corrado Senior congratulated him upon this happy coincidence and they drank another pastis.

Natalia Beaumont and Nicholas Tate, both wincing slightly, watched Marianne Lavallier's departure: an extremely sharp left turn on to the road, aided by a buffet from the right-hand gate post which was fortunately composed of solid rock; they then turned and looked at each other with raised brows.

'Well,' said Natalia, 'she's not quite the fool we've always imagined.'

Nicholas nodded thoughtfully, moving back across the room to her terrace with its beautiful view towards the sea. 'What do you think?'

'I think we'd be stupid to ignore the implications — we're not exactly overloaded with options.'

'I agree.' He glanced at his watch. 'If I pack now I can get to Nice by . . . four o'clock. Do you want to charm somebody into finding me a seat, Air France if possible?'

Madame Beaumont was surprised. 'You think it that urgent?'

'A fifth share in several million dollars? Don't you?'

'Yes, of course.'

Watching him pack his suitcase with the neatness and precision of an habitual traveller, she said, 'I don't quite see what you'll do when you get there. Where does one start?'

'One starts by securing the services of an old friend who used to be in the police force — ex-detective-inspector — now runs his own agency.'

'Can you trust him?'

'Oh my dear, yes. I know *far* too much about his private life — if you see what I mean.'

'What can I do to help?'

'Stay near the phone. If we're right, I shall certainly need you.'

*

As soon as Marianne swerved into the stable-yard she saw her son sitting on an old mounting-block eating a peach. She brought the Range-Rover to a capricious standstill and clambered out. They eyed each other warily while she smoothed her crumpled dress and he finished his peach.

'How,' he enquired, 'was Tante Natalie?'

His mother considered denial and then abandoned the idea with a shrug. 'You were fast asleep, I didn't want to wake you.'

'Nothing's ever stopped you waking me before. What was so secret this time?'

'Don't be silly!'

'What,' he continued, trying to crack the stone and get at the kernel, 'were you afraid I might tell Mademoiselle Catherine?'

She had never been able to match his quick wits in this kind of conversation. 'Well, you *are* thick with her, aren't you?'

'Me? The housekeeper's son, a *servant?*' He wasn't going to forgive her that remark in a hurry. 'I thought I was the one who was supposed to spy on her and report back to Auntie. What did you find in her bedroom?'

'Nothing.'

He stood up, tall and strong and menacing, but she had been used to this kind of man all her life and faced him squarely. Both pairs of dark eyes, so alike, were glowing with anger.

'I think,' he said evenly, 'that I'd better tell Mademoiselle you searched her room and found something so interesting you had to dash off to see Madame B. there and then.'

Abbott, returning from Toulon twenty minutes later, heard the sound of raised voices from the Lavallier house. All the same, these foreigners, far too excitable! Mother and son had both lapsed into the local patois and consequently he wasn't able to understand a word, but he was much too pleased with his afternoon's research to be bothered with those two and their arguments.

Jules Perrault. Yes, he remembered the young man well: small, dark, quick-witted, just the type to grow tired of working for a big firm and strike out on his own.

Abbott dropped into the kitchen to see that the preparation of dinner was proceeding as planned: only the three artistic gentlemen, *if* they were still on speaking terms; Madam was dining with Monsieur Gosselin and his (in Abbott's opinion) common little wife.

He was so pleased with himself that he even opened a half bottle of Edward Walden's Chambertin and savoured it luxuriously in the privacy of his monastic bedroom.

CHAPTER 4

Catherine was not used to sleeping in the afternoon, and though she had quickly fallen into the sensible Southern habit of siesta, she had never before slept so long and so soundly as upon this particular day when those around her were engaged in various ill-intentioned activities which were to have disastrous and far-reaching effects. She awoke to a feeling of disquiet, no less unpleasant for being unspecific. Shreds of some troubled dream persisted into the warm herb-scented afternoon— something to do with New York, the Subway. She had been late for an important appointment, but train after train came into the station and the doors wouldn't open for her. Other people boarded, smiling at her confusion, but she could not.

Even when she was wide awake the mood persisted. It

could hardly be caused by the knowledge that others were plotting against her, because she had known, as soon as she rejoined them after the reading of the will, after her encounter with Pascal under the bougainvillaea, that sides had been taken, the line of battle drawn up.

Pascal himself? Surely she hadn't allowed him to upset her with his games, inviting her to trust him and then telling her that she would be a fool to trust him? All meaningless, since she had *never* trusted him from the moment of their first meeting.

It certainly wasn't the onset of her period, which wasn't due for another ten days, though this feeling of a general and indeterminate malaise was its usual preface. What, then? It was true that she wasn't looking forward to dinner chez Gosselin; Madame must indeed be a virulent busybody if her own husband had to warn prospective guests to guard their tongues in front of her: which was what the lawyer had done on issuing the invitation.

She took a grip of herself, left the shady peace of her personal eyrie with its wide view down the valley, and took a swim in the pool. But there was no release even there, and not much refreshment, the water was too warm for her liking: she must ask for it to be cooled a little: enfolding her body like clinging silk instead of shocking it out of its introspective languor.

She was irritated to find that even when she had showered and dressed herself with care in her smartest dress, and taken the greatest trouble with her hair and face, and had even been reasonably satisfied with her reflection in the mirror, she was still haunted by that shadow of nagging disquiet. Very well, she must simply put up with it, she had spent most of her life putting up with much worse: her mother's tantrums, the lover's sulks or, worse, their blandishments (one had even tried to seduce her), and, when there were no more lovers, her mother's pendulum moods induced by alcohol. She grimaced at herself in the mirror and went downstairs to meet David Rudd who was partnering her to the Gosselin table.

Julie Gosselin, upon landing this rare and notable fish, had wanted to ask everybody in Montferrat who was anybody to witness her success. Monsieur Gosselin had put his foot down heavily, at which Julie had turned malicious: but *why* not Natalia Beaumont, she and the girl had already met, one could almost say that they were related; surely Mademoiselle would be *delighted* to see dear Natalia?

Since Paul Gosselin knew that his wife knew, as well as he did, why an invitation to Madame Beaumont was the crowning impossibility, he then lost his temper completely, an unusual and therefore intimidating performance, and forbade her to ask anyone else at all except Dr Sarazin and Mademoiselle Foch, the secretary, who had both attended Edward Walden in their different capacities, were both infamously reticent and therefore, as far as Julie was concerned, dull and boring.

For this reason, among others, the evening was not a success, and would indeed have been a total failure if David Rudd, like so many Englishmen of his class and upbringing, had not turned out to be an unexpected saviour of disastrous social occasions and a proficient raconteur, not in the least daunted, indeed possibly stimulated, by the recalcitrant attitude of his companions.

As he was driving her back to La Bastide, Catherine said, 'Well — thank God for you!'

Typically, he pretended not to understand her, and when she elaborated replied, 'Oh, they were sparkling company compared to the kind of thing you get at a legal dinner.'

Only upon parting did they touch upon the matter of

her affairs which affected them both so closely. When he'd pulled up in front of the house he turned to her and said, 'Satisfied with the way it's all turning out?'

'Satisfied is hardly the word. I'm staggered.' And, looking at him directly; 'I'll never be able to repay you for all your help.'

He laughed boyishly. 'Wait until you get my bill!'

Abbott had already opened the front door for her. Either he spent all his spare time watching the approach-road or some sixth sense warned him of every arrival. She said to Rudd, 'When will you be leaving?'

'Tomorrow evening, or the morning after—depending on the other ladies' lawyers, co-operative or intractable. I'll be back with all the papers within four or five days.' He glanced towards the figure at the doorway. 'Abbott behaving himself?'

'Oh yes, much quieter than I expected. I think he knows which side his bread is buttered.'

'Always has, that's his stock in trade.'

'Good night, David—and thank you again.'

'My pleasure, Madame.' He had noticed Abbott's alteration of her rank as quickly as she had. 'Bonne nuit.'

As he drove away, and as she mounted the steps of her father's house, she was aware of a distinct intensification of that disquietude which had irked her all evening. Was it her imagination, fired perhaps by David Rudd's enquiry, or was Abbott really examining her more closely than usual from under deferentially lowered lids? She thought; Oh to hell with him! To hell with them all! Within a few days I'll be rid of them, lock stock and barrel!

'Will you be requiring anything, Madam? A tisane, a cognac?'

'No, thank you, Abbott, nothing.'

'The artistic gentlemen have retired.'

'No troubles, I hope?'

'Not that I witnessed personally, but somewhere between the cheese and the sorbet the Dutch gentleman left the table and went up to his room.'

'Oh dear!'

'I fear so, Madam. Mr Edward always used to say, "Rembrandt's lady may be old but she's still a troublemaker." '

They both laughed and bade each other goodnight.

Only on reaching her bedroom did Catherine realize that she had mislaid her book. Without reading a page or two, perhaps a chapter or two, she was incapable of falling asleep. So much for habit! Now where . . . ? Yes, of course. Before slipping into that deep and troubled siesta she had tucked it under one of the cushions on the hammock. What a bore!

Within a few months, no doubt, she would have become the kind of rich girl who would, on such an occasion, promptly summon the requisite menial and ask for the book to be brought to her, but as yet such behaviour was not part of her nature. She replaced her shoes, which she had just taken off, and went down to get it herself.

Lights were always left burning inside the house, perhaps to aid the nocturnal meandering of Inspector Mattei's henchmen, and the central courtyard was also dimly lit around its perimeter. But the terrace at the base of the tower was in darkness, the moon having set or not yet risen, she was never sure which, and here, as she felt under the cushions and found the solid shape of her book, the nightmares of siesta and the general uneasiness of the evening suddenly exploded into terrifying reality.

She was just straightening up, book in hand, when the darkness stirred and she was grabbed from behind, a gloved hand tight across her mouth and a steely arm wrapped around her waist, pinning her own left arm to her side. She tried to cry out but couldn't do so; she kicked backwards, flailing with her free arm, but neither action had any effect, and to her horror she felt herself being lifted and borne forwards.

The exact meaning of the movement didn't at once strike her, she was too terrified, too intent on escape; but then the parapet at the edge of the terrace loomed up out of darkness and struck against her knees. Her knees! Was she already held up so high?

In the darkness she sensed rather than saw the sheer drop to the rocky maquis over a hundred feet below; a cooler, sweet-scented air blew up from it and turned her terror into blind panic. *She was going to be thrown over the edge!*

In panic she lashed out again with the free arm, and this time encountered a face, masked by something soft. At the same moment the strength of her assailant and the sheer lunacy of what was happening to her fused into the only possible, but impossible, solution: Pascal!

She clawed at the masked face with her fingernails. There was a grunt in her ear, and the hand which had covered her mouth was removed to grab her defensive arm. She gulped the sweet night air and screamed.

The parapet was now rough under her stomach, and in spite of darkness she realized that she was looking directly down at jagged rock. She screamed again—and several things happened at once.

There was a shout. The grip of those steely arms was momentarily slackened, and in that moment she could feel the parapet relinquishing her, she was falling. Then the most extraordinary sound, like the snarl of a lion, leapt at her right ear; she smelled the fetid breath of animal, and at the same time she was being dragged backwards, thrown forward, heaved up, dropped. Several men's voices, seeming very near, were now shouting, yelping, gasping. The parapet jumped up at her and hit her on the head, and she realized that she was no longer

held, was on her own feet, reeling, with the stone floor of
the terrace solidly beneath her.

She was still staggering. Men's bodies seemed to be
flying in all directions. The animal shot past her head
attached to one of them.

Then light snapped on, illuminating a part of the
terrace and Abbott with one hand at a switch. Images
straightened themselves out and took on recognizable or
semi-recognizable shapes. One of Inspector Mattei's men
was restraining the Doberman, running footsteps were
receding in what appeared to be all directions, and at the
same instant everything began to spin around, sliding out
of focus. She saw Abbott jumping towards her. He caught
her expertly as she fainted . . .

. . . and it was the first time in her life that she had ever
fainted. Returning consciousness told her that she was
lying on a sofa in the salon. Abbott, making a soothing,
clucking sound like a groom with a horse, was washing
her forehead with stinging antiseptic, squeezing the swab
into a bowl already richly scarlet with her blood.

Whether as a result of this sight, or of shock, or of the
head blow itself, the room faded away into a jumble of
shadows and she was flying. Or perhaps falling towards
those rocks . . .

. . . and then she was lying in her own bed (who had
undressed her?), and Dr Sarazin, looking exactly the same
as when she had last seen him at Monsieur Gosselin's
house a few hours before, was saying tetchily to someone
out of sight, 'Of course I'm sure. Police or no police, one
doesn't trifle with shock.'

Paul Gosselin now moved into her line of vision,
speaking in a faraway voice: 'But Inspector Mattei will
want to . . .'

'I'm not interested in Inspector Mattei, I'm interested

in my patient,' and he plunged a needle into her arm.

She tried to speak, but her tongue was too large for her mouth: 'Where . . . is he?'

'Where's who, my dear?' The lawyer leaned over her solicitously, kind face very concerned.

'Pas . . . Pascal.'

'Don't worry, you're quite safe, the police are looking after him.'

'Sleep,' said Dr Sarazin, bending forward in a billow of cognac fumes. 'Just sleep.'

As she drifted away again, obediently, she heard him saying, 'For God's sake, we all know that boy's mad, but . . .'

Was he mad? Catherine tried to arrange her thoughts in some kind of order, but they were resisting her. Pascal had been angry with her. When? And she had turned her back on him, pretending to be asleep.

Dr Sarazin's voice, fading: '. . . high time he was taught a damn good lesson if you ask me.'

Catherine slept.

Inspector Mattei was naturally irritated to find the victim, and only valuable source of information, lost to him in drugged stupor. Other accounts of the incident were fragmentary and inclined to contradict one another, as usual.

He inspected the scene of the attack but would not be able to carry out a proper examination until daylight. He then went to the Lavallier house where Dr Sarazin was seeing to Pascal's savaged right arm. The dog had grabbed him just below the shoulder. Marianne Lavallier watched the operation, her expression mutinous. One of Mattei's men stood in the corner, the other was still trying to pacify the Doberman, over-excited by the taste of blood; sounds of whimpering and snarling came from the stable-yard outside.

'Well,' said Mattei, 'that was a silly thing to do.'

Marianne exploded: 'You've got no right to go accusing my boy without the . . .'

'Madame, would you be so kind as to leave the room?'

'No, I wouldn't.' In these ancient hill communities there was little respect for Toulonnais in general and Toulon policemen in particular. Mattei was perfectly used to such women; he shrugged and turned back to Pascal. 'Young men don't attack girls for no reason. Do you want to make a statement?'

Pascal did not reply.

'You'll have to make one in the end. If you want a lawyer to be present, Monsieur Gosselin is just along the corridor.'

Pascal winced at Dr Sarazin's less than tender ministrations but still didn't speak.

'Oh, for God's sake,' said his mother, 'tell the Inspector. Stop playing games!'

Mattei passed a hand over his sleek head and sighed. 'The usual motive in such cases is sexual, or at least emotional, but since the lady is your half-sister . . .'

Pascal shook his head pityingly. 'With me it's different. I just like to go around scaring girls out of their wits, it's a kind of habit.'

'Pascal!' The usual warning from his mother.

'Scaring doesn't enter into it,' said the Inspector. 'By all accounts this was attempted murder.'

Pascal gave him one of his darker looks. 'By all accounts? By whose account? Does Mademoiselle think I attacked her?'

'Yes, she does.'

The young man's eyes betrayed a moment's stark incredulity, and then anger. 'Shit! She said that to you?'

'Not to me personally, she's under sedation. She said it to Monsieur Gosselin and the Doctor here.' He was interested to note the degree of feeling which this had aroused; and hastened to capitalize on it. 'There are only two entrances to La Bastide, the main door and the gate to the stable-yard. Both are locked at night and the outward-facing windows on the ground floor are all barred; and more or less impossible to reach anyway. Therefore no outsider could have entered. Therefore the criminal was already inside, Do you follow me?'

'Perfectly.' He had conquered the anger and regained some of his insolent poise.

'Monsieur Lavallier, you'd do well to tell me the truth. Otherwise I shall jump to the obvious conclusion.'

'Is there one?'

'You know there is. Owing to the very existance of Mademoiselle Walden you and your mother find yourselves cut out of your father's will—am I correct?'

Pascal nodded. The doctor had finished with his arm.

'You were naturally infuriated when you learned of this. You're known to be a young man of violent and unstable temper . . .' He gestured.

'Well,' said Pascal, 'it's not a bad story.'

Marianne could contain herself no longer. 'What's the *matter* with you? You behave as if it was some kind of debt of honour, and it's nothing of the sort. If you won't speak up and tell him the truth, I will.'

Natalia Beaumont's reaction upon seeing her own son, the usually immaculate copybook Lieutenant, pale but elated, covered in dust and twigs, standing on her doorstep at Montferrat, with blood pouring from some kind of a wound in his arm, well after midnight, was one of horror tempered by a practical knowledge of his character and the historical behaviour of her family.

Of course he ought to be three hundred miles away in Besançon, fast asleep, or carousing in the Mess, or going about his military duties. But as a small boy of eight he had disappeared into the maquis for three days and nights to see if he could 'live like a Red Indian', and at twelve he had made his way to Toulon in order to sign on as a cabin-boy. And had not her Russian grandfather been the last man, reputedly, to fight a duel in the Bois de Boulogne, though the seconds had possessed enough sense to load both revolvers with blanks.

However, her reaction upon hearing what he'd *done* was altogether different; mere horror, as well as motherly concern for his safety, were swept away by a torrent of impatience and anger. 'Oh God, no! I don't believe it.'

'I wanted to give her a jolly good shock, you see, maybe scare her out of the place. Then I remembered what a ninny she was about heights. I used to tease her—remember?—that time she came to stay.'

'Are you *crazy?*'

'A bit, I suppose. You always say I am.'

His complacency was the last straw. She lost her temper. 'Jean-Michel, Nicky Tate and I are in the middle of a very awkward, very delicate transaction which *could* justify all our claims to your father's estate, and you . . . you come blundering in and endanger the whole thing with this stupid, childish . . .'

He was staring at her, not understanding a word.

'Don't you see? If anybody recognized you . . .'

'Nobody did, they went after Pascal.' He said this with such clod-hopping self-satisfaction that in a flash she understood the whole thing: his primary concern had not been to frighten Catherine at all, because even by his disjointed methods of reasoning such an action could have no lasting effect, could even have an opposite effect, on a young woman of character. Oh no, he had planned to do something violent and foolish for which Pascal, the hated and despised half-brother, would automatically be blamed. And why? Because Pascal had openly mocked him by using his name when in dubious pursuit of that same young woman, and had compounded the infamy by punching Jean-Michel in the solar plexus at the reading of the will. It made no rational sense whatsoever, which was why Natalia, a rational woman, knew it at once for the truth.

While she washed and dressed the injured arm (mercifully it was no more than a gash which could easily be accounted for and hidden under a uniform) she contained her anger, which she knew to be useless anyway, and listened to the details of his idiotic plan.

'You see, it only takes three and a half hours by the autoroute in a decent car, of course you have to allow quite a bit for the last part because of the mountains — so I borrowed this Porsche off one of the chaps. It really was a terrific drive, I averaged a hundred between Vienne and Orange . . .'

Yes, she could see it all with blistering clarity: the boyish face taut in concentration, wind whipping the fair hair, quick blue eyes assessing every possibility of danger, both on the road itself and from waiting police. He would probably have made an excellent racing-driver; he would be capable, if trained, of teetering across Niagara Falls on a wire; he enjoyed scuba-diving, free-fall parachuting. In short he was given to the kind of pursuits which she, in her own youth, had found ridiculous and exasperating, and by God she found them even more ridiculous and exasperating now!

'. . . and then, you see, I'd have hopped in the car and been back in quarters long before Reveillé, I'd probably have got an hour or two's sleep.' He glanced at his Rolex. 'I'll still make it easily, but without the sleep.'

He recounted the whole hair-raising performance as if it was part of some film he'd seen, and well it might be. He was removed from it, uninvolved even though exhilarated.

Yes, Natalia thought wearily, he probably *would* distinguish himself in action, when and if he had to face it; he would probably end up being the youngest Colonel or General or whatever. Unless . . .

'But are you *sure* nobody recognized you?'

'With this over my face?' A thin woollen stocking. 'Anyway, I'm three hundred miles away, aren't I?'

'They could telephone.'

'François would say I was around somewhere, he'd say we'd been out together.'

'But what does François think?'

'That I'm in bed with a married woman. He'd never let me down, I'd do the same for him.'

'I hope you're right.'

'Of course I am. Mother, do stop worrying!'

Realizing that he had not at all understood the terrible harm which he might have done, she took him by both shoulders and said, with all the patience she could muster, 'Promise me, *promise* me not to do anything else — we may survive this one if we're lucky.'

'Oh come on! It was only a kind of joke.'

'The kind of joke that lands people in prison. And another thing: if *she* finds out . . .'

'Who cares if she does?'

'Jean, we may fail to establish any rights regarding that will — in which case we're reliant entirely on her generosity.'

'Good God no! I'll never allow that.'

Natalia made a wide gesture with both arms, as if committing herself to the mercy of heaven, and gave up. She found him a slice of quiche and a glass of cognac; then sat down while he ate and drank, willing herself to be quiet, to be calm.

Munching, 'Where's Nicholas? I thought he was here.'

'He's gone back to London.' She didn't mention the reason for Nicholas's sudden departure, she wanted her darling boy out of the house, back in Besançon. She had now succeeded in curbing her anger completely; it meant

nothing to him, and only succeeded in exhausting her.
'Supposing the police are watching the roads?'
'They won't be, they've got Pascal. I say, it was a bit of
luck his coming to her rescue, wasn't it? You might have
told me they were using dogs.'
'Jean, I wasn't to know you proposed a visit, let alone
one as . . . unexpected as this. Pascal will tell them it was
you.'
'They won't believe him, nobody believes Pascal.' He
gulped down the rest of the brandy and stood up. 'And
don't worry about the police, I'll take the back road.'
'And go to the doctor when you get there, you can tell
him your married lady's dog surprised you.'
He enjoyed this; climbed, laughing, into the Porsche;
roared away into the night, into silence. His mother gazed
after him, shaking her head.

At La Bastide, Catherine slumbered peacefully, a
policeman outside her door. Pascal, guarded by another
policeman, lay on his bed fully dressed, awake and
glowering. Inspector Mattei had been given one of the
guest suites. He had listened attentively to Marianne's
allegations regarding Lieutenant Jean-Michel Beaumont;
it was a far-fetched story but then, God knows, this was a
far-fetched family.
Out of curiosity he telephoned Lieutenant Beaumont's
unit at Besançon, and was presently connected to a
Lieutenant François de Noyers who said that he had been
with his friend Jean-Michel all evening at a rather good
party. Well, no — as a matter of fact Jean-Michel was at
the moment otherwise engaged, having escorted an
attractive lady to her home. No doubt he'd be back in
quarters presently, would the Inspector like him to call?
Mattei, who knew a set-up when he met one, which he
did every day, sometimes three or four times a day, said
No, it wasn't important. At the moment it wasn't. If

Mademoiselle Walden wanted to prefer charges, things would be rather different, but the Inspector knew enough about the army to realize that its code of honour was exactly the same as that of the 'milieu'. Officers and gentlemen, like crooks and rogues, didn't betray friends.

All in all he found it an interesting situation, and he might, as was his habit, be able to make some private capital out of it, but otherwise it very much looked as if it was going to turn into an impasse. One didn't worry about impasses, one slept on them.

CHAPTER 5

Catherine awoke to find herself feeling less battered than she had expected. Shock had left her shaky, of course, and she appeared to be bruised and stiff in many unexpected places, but her head ached hardly at all, while the mirror revealed that the cut was minimal in spite of all that blood. The attendant bruise could be hidden by a rearrangement of her hair.

News from the outside world was promising. The artistic gentlemen had departed to confer with their several authorities; others were to arrive next day, among them Sotheby's various experts. Meanwhile it was unfortunately necessary for her to see devious Inspector Mattei and to face the whole matter of Pascal; she wasn't looking forward to either.

Mattei had spent half an hour examining the terrace. Not that it took him more than a few minutes to find what he was looking for: what Madame Lavallier's extraordinary statement in defence of her son had led him to expect. On the northern side of the tower, which would have been in darkness even after Abbott had turned on the light, just where the edging wall of the terrace met the first of the buildings which formed the quadrangle of La Bastide, the stone was scored with several groups of scratches; at one point these came to an end immediately beneath a slightly protruding piece of masonry.

Somebody had stood among the rocks below and had flung a grappling-hook over the wall, more than once, until the lip of stone gave it a firm hold; this person had then climbed the cliff-face and reached the terrace. The grappling-hook was a standard article of military equipment, much used by commandos and suchlike daredevils, and the climb, though intimidating to the average civilian, or indeed policeman, would be child's play to a trained soldier.

Mattei's dog-handler had seen only one man attacking the girl and, he thought, Abbott going to her assistance. Abbott, however, said that he had not moved towards her until she fainted. The other policeman had seen two men attacking the girl, but to Mattei it was now obvious that the second had been Pascal, not Abbott, defending her. The wretched dog could hardly be blamed for not knowing who was doing what.

The next move, according to the book, was to contact colleagues in Besançon, who would determine (a) exactly where Lieutenant Beaumont had been last night, i.e. in whose bed, and (b) whether he was in any way wounded, probably in the right arm since police dogs were trained to go for the right arm. Inspector Mattei had little doubt as to the results of such an enquiry; on the other hand he had grave doubts as to their legal value, and even graver doubts regarding their all-important usefulness to himself. Certain information tended to be more profitable if kept private.

Like the canny Corsican he was, Mattei possessed a valuable savings account of such information. Even when it didn't pay interest, and in the end it usually did, the very knowledge of its existence gave him a satisfactory sense of power. He loved power, not only as a beautiful object in its own right but because, as an ambitious policeman, he knew that it paved the way to promotion.

So, standing at the end of Catherine's bed, he came straight to the point. 'Mademoiselle, I believe you suspect Pascal Lavallier of this assault.'

'I . . . What else can I . . . ? Yes.'

Knowing from the hesitant answer as well as from the unhappy face what she would reply, he added, 'Then you wish to bring charges against him?'

'Well . . . No, I don't.' And more defiantly: 'After all, he's my half-brother.'

'Also a good-for-nothing young rascal.'

'I don't agree.' Said with too much feeling.

Mattei smiled. Something rich and strange here all right: the silence of the boy, the defiant protectiveness of the girl. Yes indeed, a *very* far-fetched family! 'On such occasions the police themselves often bring a case.'

'I . . . Naturally I can't stop you. But I'd rather you didn't.'

'May I commend you, Mademoiselle, on your family loyalty.'

She flushed, and her fine eyes were full of anger, but she managed to say, 'Thank you. It's . . . the least I can do.'

As the Inspector drove down the valley towards Montferrat he thought, not for the first time, that there was never any harm in holding a stock of secret knowledge about rich families. Even if Mademoiselle Walden's defence of her good-looking half-brother was not what he suspected, it could very easily be made to look like it if such a recourse ever became profitable.

He found Natalia Beaumont in her smart little sitting-room. A smart little suitcase lay open on the sofa; she was just putting her address-book and various papers into it.

A coat, matching her smart suit, was draped over the arm of a nearby chair.

'I'm sorry to intrude. Madame is going away?'

'To London, to visit friends for a day or two.' Nicholas Tate had telephoned early that morning, summoning her urgently.

Mattei understood that her departure probably had nothing to do with her son's activities of the preceding night, but an implied connection was inevitable, increasing Madame's controlled but evident nervousness and therefore his command of the situation. He said, 'How fortunate that I arrived before you left. May I ask when you last saw Lieutenant Beaumont?'

He had always admired strong-minded women; they were interesting to interrogate, providing a nice sharp battle of wills. Shrinking violets he abhorred; they brought out the sadistic worst in him.

'He managed to get twenty-four hours' leave for the reading of his father's will. That would have been five, no, six days ago.'

'You've heard that Mademoiselle Walden was attacked last night.'

'I've already sent my condolences. What a perfectly appalling thing to happen in a . . .' The look of dawning outrage was faultlessly contrived, he could almost believe it. 'You aren't implying . . . Inspector, why are you here?'

'The fact is, Madame, it's been suggested that your son was responsible.'

'Suggested? The Lavalliers, I suppose — what absolute rubbish!'

Yes, she was really very good; it took a Frenchwoman to do it well; the girl, though strong, would never master such attack, such timing. 'You're not telling me *Mademoiselle* has accused my son.'

'No. She suspects Pascal Lavallier.'

'As well she might. Charges?'

'She prefers not to bring them—against her own half-brother.'

'How admirable!' She invited him to share the sarcasm but he declined. Looking out of the window, he said, 'I understand that because she was sole beneficiary in her father's will, Mademoiselle has made . . . very generous allowances for the rest of the family, if I may call it that.'

His insolence enraged her, but she contained herself admirably. 'Yes.'

'You and your son are included in this generosity, of course.'

'We are.'

'So that if she ever discovered that Lieutenant Beaumont *was* responsible for that attack . . .'

Silence. He turned his head and found her staring at him with wide eyes, not knowing quite what to reply, quite what attitude to adopt. He could hardly blame her, these swift Corsican knife-thrusts were one of his favourite methods of attack. Typically, Madame Beaumont chose as sharp a method for her defence. 'Mademoiselle's reaction could hardly be more outraged than that of your superiors if I reported that you had used blackmail. Or did I perhaps misunderstand you?'

He laughed. 'I don't believe we have either of us misunderstood the other, Madame. It's a pleasure to talk to such an intelligent woman.' Since it was always advisable to make doubly sure of an adversary as spry as this, he added, 'My goodness, what a story they'd make of it in . . . say, *France Dimanche!*'

'There is no story, Inspector, merely a number of impertinent assumptions on your part.'

' "Illegitimate Half-Brothers Battle For Sister's Love." ' He managed to make it sound perfectly ridiculous; the light touch didn't come to him naturally, but he had taught himself its uses; as here, for the chilling of a strong woman's blood. Finis to her darling boy's career!

'Newspapers don't court libel actions unless they have absolute proof.'

'They don't *print* such stories, Madame, unless they have absolute proof.'

She was eyeing him guardedly. He guessed that since he had now made himself quite clear, they were about to reach bed-rock. 'It seems to me, Inspector, that you're suggesting, if clumsily, some kind of . . . understanding between us. I don't have much time—perhaps you'd be so good as to tell me exactly what you want.'

'Intelligent *and* straightforward! I don't ask much, Madame, I'm only a rather humble policeman. If, at some time in the future, you're ever able to . . . introduce me to any interesting possibilities . . .' He gestured.

'Favouring your career, is that what you mean?'

'One's superiors are always demanding what they call "results".'

'Hm!' She looked at her suitcase, frowning. 'As a matter of fact I may be able to do exactly that. It's not certain but . . . quite possible, yes.'

'Don't hesitate to call on me, Madame—here's my number.'

Madame Beaumont put the card in her handbag and snapped it shut. 'My son was last at Monferrat six days ago.'

'Then I shall naturally close that line of enquiry.' He hadn't enjoyed an interview so much for years.

Dr Sarazin kept Catherine in bed all day, partly because he mistrusted the after-effects of shock and partly because the matter of Pascal's guilt had not yet been resolved. Neither he nor Monsieur Gosselin felt like taking any chances where that extraordinary young man was concerned.

However, following his interesting conversation with Natalia Beaumont, Inspector Mattei considered that the

time was ripe for him to issue an 'official explanation' of
the incident, an explanation allowing each person
concerned to make of it what they willed, which of course
meant what suited them best.

Mademoiselle Walden, on going down to the terrace to
find her book, had been surprised by an intruder who had
gained access to La Bastide by climbing the cliff with the
aid of a grappling-hook, a means of entry implying
considerable professional expertise: in fact a practised
burglar. The 'milieu' of Toulon and Marseille had always
known about Edward Walden's art treasures, naturally,
and interest had been re-aroused by the many newspaper
accounts of his death, all of which had mentioned the
collection. Catherine's screams had alerted Pascal
Lavallier as well as Abbott and Mattei's own men. All
four had rushed to her aid. Unfortunately the police dog,
bemused by the fracas, had grabbed Pascal instead of the
intruder who had disappeared into the night, escaping as
he had arrived.

The doctor, the lawyer and the victim herself received
this analysis with varying degrees of relief, the Lavalliers
mother and son with unconcealed contempt. To them, in
private, the Inspector added that he had made enquiries
at Besançon and that Lieutenant Beaumont had been in
the company of friends all that evening. If, he added with
emphasis, they both considered the matter carefully, they
would appreciate that everything had turned out for the
best, since they had all been omitted from Edward
Walden's will and all stood to gain from the generosity
and goodwill of his daughter.

Marianne said in good round country terms what she
thought of this hocus-pocus, eliciting a thin smile from
Mattei, but Pascal kept his thoughts to himself.

At last free to go wherever he wished, he was infuriated
to find that a policeman was still on duty outside
Catherine's bedroom door, denying all access; perhaps

even more infuriated by the strength of his desire to speak to her. His wounded arm was hurting him a good deal, though Dr Sarazin, in a gentler frame of mind now that the young man had been exonorated, said that it was coming along nicely and advised him to rest. Rest!

Next day, Catherine appeared, looking pale but perfectly self-possessed. She immediately went into conference with Monsieur Gosselin, a lengthy discussion concerning the sale of the estate. More art experts arrived in time for luncheon, so that Pascal was obliged to bide his time yet longer, prowling about the garden, nursing his thoughts. And then, just as the lawyer was about to depart, and long after Abbott, dapper in pale grey, had driven away to do whatever it was that he did on his afternoons off, the doctor returned to see that Mademoiselle was not over-exerting herself. Monsieur Gosselin thereupon lingered, and all three settled down for another cup of coffee. Pascal beat his forehead gently against the rough stone wall of the tower.

Abbott drove carefully into Nice. The autoroute, particularly after the Cannes turn-off, was always monopolized by maniacs. He found Monsieur Perrault's establishment without difficulty. It was not, as he had expected, a small builder's yard but a thriving Do-It-Yourself emporium situated in the kind of neat but not wealthy suburb where most of the husbands would be likely to spend most of their weekends doing it themselves: whether they were assembling Jules Perrault's pre-packaged garden tables, his easy-fit bookshelves, his wide range of barbecue machinery.

Madame Perrault, an attractive and beady little woman who was obviously determined to make her husband affluent or die in the attempt, presided over the cash, and Jules himself offered technical advice or explained to the more obtuse customers that their inability to master the super-simple-assembly garden bench lay in the fact that they had bolted Bar X to stanchion Y and should re-read the enclosed instructions.

He had been warned by his old employer in Toulon of Abbott's impending visit. They retired to the yard to escape from importunate customers. Monsieur Perrault scratched his head and admitted that what with one thing and another — setting up in your own business was no holiday — he had more or less forgotten that job at La Bastide and the exact position of the hot water pipes beneath the floorboards.

'To tell you the truth,' said Abbott, 'I didn't entirely take old Corrado into my confidence. You know what they're like in Toulon . . .' He had remembered that Jules Perrault himself was a Niçois and proud of it. 'They gossip a lot, don't they? And between you and me this is rather a private matter.'

'Don't worry, Mr Abbott, I don't have any time for chit-chat even if it was in my nature. What's your problem?'

'I'd like you to cast your mind back to the time you carried out that work — November of last year, unless I'm much mistaken . . .'

Paul Gosselin and the doctor had departed, and the mandarins of the art world, Monsieur Delaroche of the Louvre at last making a tardy appearance, and two more superior Oxbridges from Sotheby's in London, had repaired to different parts of the house to brood upon values. Catherine, whose head was aching a little, had dozed off beside the pool when, as before, she became aware of the fact that she was not alone and, as before, opened her eyes to find Pascal regarding her, but on this occasion with an anger which was all the more intense for having been bottled up during so many hours of waiting. 'Is what they say true? Do you really think I'd do that? To *you?*'

Catherine recognized the anger with misgiving, but was neither surprised nor intimidated. 'Yes, I did. Now I owe you an apology. I'm sorry.'

'You're *sorry!* So that makes everything okay, doesn't it? La Grande Mademoiselle has deigned to apologize to the housekeeper's son. Big deal!'

Catherine regarded him in silence, frowning. There could be one reason only for this bitter rage; it didn't enter into her plans and she was unwilling to accept it. Pascal, however, was determined to have his say: 'You know how I feel about you, I've told you, I've shown you!' He took a pace forward, bending so near that his fury pinned her to the sun-bed on which she was lying. 'And you think *I*'d jump out at you in the dark and scare you half to death — you must be mad!'

Catherine had recoiled in so far as her position allowed her to do so. 'I . . . There's no other word except "sorry", is there? I thought it was another of those games you're so good at, and you were angry with me that afternoon, and . . . I couldn't think who else it could be — that strong, inside La Bastide.' She managed to stand up, putting the awkward piece of garden furniture between them. Now, please! I've apologized, let's drop the whole thing, let's cool it.'

'Cool it! Why?'

'You know why.'

'Tell me something. Remember the day you saw me here in the garden?'

The apparently naked figure, abruptly disappearing, she wasn't likely to forget. 'Yes.'

'Remember how Mother appeared and told you I was her son?'

After a moment, her face stony, Catherine said, 'Yes.'

'Remember how angry you were? You shouted at me . . .'

'I was being silly.'

'You called me disgusting and perverted.'

'I don't think . . . I'm sure I didn't.'

'You did. Why perverted, Catherine?'

'Obviously. That was when I realized that we were . . . so closely related—and you'd had the gall to make love to me!'

'But all you knew was that I was Madame Lavallier's son, you didn't know *he* was my father.'

She stared at him in silence.

'You didn't know until old Natalia told you a few hours later—remember how shocked you were?—when she and Nicky and Monsieur Gosselin came up to lecture you about the will. Yes, I was listening, I always do.'

Silence. A breath of wind rippled the pool and was drowned at the far end of it.

'Maybe I'm not the only one who plays games.'

Her tension broke. She let out her breath and waved a dismissive hand, turning away from him. 'All right, I *did* know. My mother told me he'd had a couple of illegitimate sons, by her friend Natalia and by his housekeeper. If I chose to keep it to myself that's my business.'

'Ah!' He went after her quickly, facing her again. 'So when we were kissing under the trees at Lapalisse you already knew I was your half-brother!'

'How could I? You'd lied to me about your name.' He hadn't thought of that one; *his* turn to be silent. She continued at once: 'If you'd told me you were called Pascal Lavallier, of course I'd have known. But you didn't.' Again she turned away, this time picking up her book and a sweater preparatory to leaving him.

He came up behind her. As at their first meeting, in her car, she could feel the heat of his body and its magnetism. Quietly now, he said, 'I'm sorry I shouted at you.'

'And I'm sorry I thought for one second that you could

do . . . that cruel thing. It was . . . stupid of me.'

He laughed. 'Know what? We've just had a lovers' quarrel.'

She turned on him then and gave him the coldest of cold grey looks. 'No, Pascal, we have not.'

'Yes, Catherine, we have. Why pretend? We both know, we're so alike.'

She wheeled away, heart pounding, and left him standing there, smiling at her retreating back.

All she needed after this was a lengthy dinner with Monsieur Delaroche of the Louvre and the two Sothebys who would go on and on and on about craquelure and authentication and provenance. Luckily she had every excuse for eating alone in her suite and retiring to bed early, and this she did, waited on, in Abbott's absence, by gentle Isabelle with whom she felt entirely at home.

Abbott, meanwhile, was celebrating his extremely successful day, a true red-letter day, by dining at his favourite restaurant, one of the best in Nice, where he was treated like a lord: possibly because he had encouraged the proprietor and his staff, by princely tips and a princely manner, to think he was one.

Afterwards he would perhaps visit Sophie, a plump whore of his acquaintance, who would put on a pair of long black boots and take off everything else, and then chastise him pitilessly with one of her delectable collection of whips. That concluded (it didn't take long), he would buy himself a nice box of chocolates and go to a cinema which, he had noticed when driving through the town, was showing a double bill: two old and sentimental American musicals, both of which he had seen many times before and would certainly see many times again. Sophie was a necessary convenience, but sentimental musicals and a good box of chocolates, those were true ecstasy.

CHAPTER 6

On the following day, a day she was to remember in minutest detail for the rest of her life, Catherine took breakfast in her room, with the intention of avoiding Pascal who would doubtless be lurking like a young satyr in the leafy shadows of the garden. This time it was Abbott who attended her, wearing the pale blue linen jacket which constituted his morning uniform.

After she had eaten her croissants he returned to see if she required fresh coffee, and even though she said, 'No, thank you, there's still some in the pot,' he seemed inclined to hover, so that she was forced to add: 'Yes, Abbott?'

'Madam, I find this somewhat embarrassing, but a . . . significant and I fear awkward circumstance has been brought to my attention.'

The rotund phrasing and the averted eyes warned her that the circumstance in question was unpleasant. Was he about to display some of that malicious insubordination which he had recently been holding in check?—and so soon after she had assured David Rudd that he was behaving himself. 'Tell me.'

'Well, Madam, I happened to go into Toulon to query a bill for some work done to the house a few months before your father's death.'

'And?' Was she going to have to drag every sentence out of him?

'In the course of my enquiries I found myself talking to one of the labourers employed on the job. This was in November, Madam, at the time of Mr Rudd's last visit to Mr Edward.'

Catherine took another sip of the excellent coffee, her

last in fact, though she had by no means finished it.

'He told me that on a certain day, the fifteenth to be precise — he remembers it because it was his wife's birthday and he was afraid he might be detained and spoil the party they'd arranged — and incidentally it was a Wednesday, my day off, which is why I knew nothing about it . . . Well, Madam, on this day Mr Rudd called him and his colleague into Mr Edward's room and asked them if they would be so kind as to witness a will which he had just drawn up. Mr Edward, ah . . . signed it in their presence.'

Silence. Catherine continued to stare, mouth slightly open, cup poised. Abbott glanced away; cleared his throat as if to add something to this stupendous bombshell; then decided not to say it.

Catherine put down the cup with a clatter. 'But . . . But I don't understand. Mr Rudd said . . . You heard him . . . Abbott, he said he'd discussed a second will with my father, and my father had done nothing about it.'

'Yes, Madam, I remember very clearly.'

She put a hand over her eyes for a moment; then stood up abruptly. 'What does it mean? For God's sake, Mr Rudd can't have been *lying!*'

'One would hesitate to jump to such a conclusion, Madam, but . . .' He gestured, indicating that there were not many other conclusions within jumping distance.

Catherine was now pacing about the room in a fury of agitation. 'No, no — it's impossible. It *must* be impossible, Abbott, mustn't it? I mean . . . you know Mr Rudd better than I do.'

'A very nice gentleman, Madam, very correct. An old and trusted friend of Mr Edward's.'

'I must speak to him at once, there may be some quite simple explanation. Perhaps my father changed his mind a few minutes later and tore up the will.'

'Perhaps, Madam.'

'Oh God, supposing Mr Rudd's already left for Paris!'

But a telephone call to the hotel banished this fear. David Rudd had been detained in Marseille the day before, had returned late, was catching a plane at midday, was still in his room and had asked not to be disturbed before ten.

'I'm sorry about that. Please put me through, it's very urgent.'

Abbott was making sidling movements towards the door, but Catherine held up a hand to restrain him; it was obviously vital, in the context, that he heard everything.

'David? Catherine — I'm sorry to wake you, I . . . Abbott has just told me something quite extraordinary. I think . . . I'd rather not discuss it on the phone, we must meet at once.'

She listened, tapping her foot impatiently. 'But that'll be a waste of time, it's quicker for me to come to the hotel while you get up and shave.' The voice on the other end of the line was becoming less lethargic, more alert. 'No I don't know it but I can easily find it. La Réserve, yes. I'll be there in . . . what, half an hour?'

She banged down the receiver and looked at the manservant, who again averted those washed-out blue eyes, shrugging his narrow shoulders. 'I can only hope that there's some mistake, Madam, though the man seemed quite sure of what he told me.'

'We'll soon find out. I must dress.' And, as he turned to go: 'Abbott, I know that Madame Beaumont held a meeting at her house, to do with me and the will. I know that you were there.'

'Not entirely at my own wish.'

'I must ask you — please don't mention this to anyone else. I'll tell you what Mr Rudd says as soon as I get back. Better still, he'll probably tell you himself.'

'Very good, Madam. Shall I have a car brought to the

door, the Range Rover perhaps?'

'No, my little Renault. And Abbott — without Pascal
Lavallier knowing, if possible.'

'He's out in the vineyard, Madam, with the factor.'

La Réserve was one of those exclusive hostelries which still
manage to exist amid the chaos which is all that's left of
the French Riviera: in this case because it was wedged
between an intractable bastion of rock and a large area of
private land. Catherine found it with some difficulty.
David Rudd was pacing to and fro on a white-painted
wooden terrace above a Mediterranean dotted with the
bright sails of windsurfers and little yachts. Against this
jolly background, a modern Dufy, they met with grim
faces.

'Abbott knows there's a second will.'

'God in heaven! How?'

Natalia Beaumont could have told him how. As she
had said to Nicholas after the meeting at her house,
'Abbott's up to something. I saw him change, right in the
middle of a sentence. Something struck him, something
we all missed.'

Rudd swore explicitly. 'But he wasn't even *there*, it was
his day off.'

'So you said. But he's found one of those builders you
called in to witness it.'

'What the hell put him on to them?'

'I've no idea.'

The answer was: a simple process of elimination. It was
Marianne Lavallier, at that meeting, who had pointed
out that if there'd been a will there would also have had to
be witnesses; and Abbott himself had quickly discounted
the staff of La Bastide because each of them could expect
to receive some kind of legacy; as for outsiders, he had
said, 'If anybody came to visit him I knew about it. They
didn't, not any strangers.'

Was this the very moment at which Natalia Beaumont had noticed the change in him? The moment at which he had remembered the only possible strangers: Monsieur Corrado's men, at that time repairing the floor of the long gallery?

'What are we going to *do*, David?'

Catherine had always known, because her mother had told her several times, that Edward Walden's lawyers were Mayer, Rudd and Wilson in London. It had seemed only sensible to visit them, following the news of her father's death, before going on to Montferrat. She had accordingly booked her flight via London instead of directly to Nice.

David Rudd had received her in his imposing panelled office with the portrait of his grandfather in judge's robes over the fireplace; and he had instantly shattered all her hopes. 'Miss Walden, I'm sorry to have to tell you this, but . . . You must know that your parents didn't speak to each other for years.'

'Of course I know. I can't blame him — from his point of view she behaved appallingly.'

'Yes, well . . . that's as may be.' Mr Rudd, who knew better than she did how appallingly her father had also behaved, was not about to sit in judgement. 'In that case you probably won't be surprised to hear that he cut her out of his will entirely.'

'Surprised, no — but I . . .' He saw understanding take possession of her face; saw it crumple before his eyes. 'You mean . . . ? You can't mean . . .'

'I'm afraid so. He cut you out too. I argued with him, I told him it was cruel, unfair, but . . .' He sighed. 'I truly am most awfully sorry.'

Catherine would never forget that moment, the sense of falling into a bottomless chasm. Ever since visiting La Bastide, or more properly ever since seeing the article about it in *House and Garden*, she had comforted herself in her moments of utmost misery and loneliness with the thought that one day it would belong to her because she was Edward Walden's only legitimate child. She knew about the two little bastard boys, her mother had regaled her with every detail of their conception, birth and ensuing history, and she had accustomed herself to the idea that she would very possibly have to share her inheritance with them and with their respective mothers; in her opinion there was nothing wrong with that, it was perfectly fair. *But to be excluded altogether!*

David Rudd, afraid that she might be about to pass out in his office — not the first to do so — swiftly poured a glass of brandy and put it on the table beside her. But she was made of stronger stuff than those others; shook her head; even managed to dredge up a wan smile by way of thanks. 'That means . . . my two . . . half-brothers get it all.'

'With their mothers, yes. Shocking, I agree, but then Edward was in many ways a shocker. And towards the end he . . . He was in pain, of course, he became strangely, uncharacteristically . . . yes, vindictive, it's the right word.' He pushed back the lock of hair and went on talking, his aim being to give her time to recover from the blow, never dreaming what would arise from his words. 'It's only a minor indication, of course, but in my own case . . . One had reason to think that after seventeen years, and he wasn't the easiest of clients . . . some small legacy — I'm not being venal, you understand, it's the usual thing, an acknowledgement of faithful service. And of course he knew all about my wife's illness, an enormous drain on one's resources. But no. He said, "I hope *you're* not expecting largesse, Davey, you've made quite enough out of me already, I find your fees excessive." Of course he was joking, half-joking, but it wasn't the Edward Walden I'd known for so long. Waspish. Yes, vindictive. One of my wife's specialists tells me it often affects them that way. Poor Edward!'

Catherine was not aware of assimilating all this at the time. In fact it was not until half an hour later, when she was walking along the Strand, unseeing, almost unknowing, lost in a black valley of disappointment, that the lawyer's words penetrated into her consciousness.

She came to a halt, staring into space. Passers-by glanced at the beautiful, rapt face, wondering whether she was quite right in the head.

After a time she turned and began to walk slowly back towards the office: slowly at first and then more quickly until she was all but running. There had been a nice friendly girl at the reception desk and the reception desk was on the ground floor, whereas Mayer, Rudd and Wilson occupied the third and fourth floors, safely removed.

She said, 'I feel I ought to write to Mr Rudd, to offer him my sympathy—about his wife.'

'Oh yes.' The extrovert London face pinched itself into lines of woe. 'Poor Mrs Rudd, such a lovely person too!'

'But you see, coming from New York only this morning, I don't really know . . .'

The British love of a nice disaster made further discreet enquiry unnecessary. Between the receiving of other visitors and the connecting of various telephone calls, the girl willingly recounted the whole piteous story of Mary Rudd's misfortunes.

'Three operations, how appalling! And the expense! But of course you have your wonderful National Health scheme.'

'No, that's just it—the Health said there was a year's waiting, and then there were more strikes, and Mr Rudd couldn't *allow* her to wait, could he? So it's all been done Private, and goodness knows what it's cost him! Half punchy with worry he's been at times, it's awful, it really is, and him so nice, the nicest man I ever worked for, no kidding.'

Catherine took this back with her to her hotel, aligned it with Mr Rudd's own bitter words, and brooded upon it all at length; viewed it from every angle; slept on it, finally, and awoke resolved. The fact was that she had nothing to lose because everything was already lost. She picked up the telephone and made another appointment with her father's lawyer.

His face as he listened to her was blank with a kind of outraged disbelief; not that she gave it more than a couple of swift and horrified glances. Yes, horrified; she was as appalled at what she heard herself saying as he undoubtedly was to hear it being said. And yet he didn't stop her, ask her to leave his office at once. She could feel an intermittent, extremely faint but none the less distinct current of interest emanating from him, and he didn't refuse to answer her few questions, even if the voice in which he replied sounded breathless, stunned.

When she had finished, had laid the whole preposterous idea before him, he was silent. For a very long time he stared at her, frowning; then he blew out his breath as if he had been holding it for the past fifteen minutes, and pushed back the boyish lock of hair; then he pushed it back again and turned away from her, looking out of the window at the ancient square where four generations of his family had followed their complicated profession with honour and distinction: generally speaking, his Uncle Tom had been a bit of a rascal.

Meanwhile Catherine sat very still, examining her hands. She felt a great calm, like a gambler who has staked everything on one spin of the wheel and now has nothing to do but wait for the little ball to come to rest, obliterating hope or permitting it to rise phoenix-like from disaster. Despite her dislocated upbringing, she had striven to live as honestly and straightforwardly as the world allowed. But she supposed that there came moments, or a moment, in most people's lives when they encountered a fence which good old Honesty, that weary nag, refused to jump. And this, in her life, was it. In David Rudd's life also? Still he didn't speak.

And when finally he did, he took her completely by surprise. Initially. Later she understood that it was a sensible and lawyer-like reply. 'Miss Walden, could you dine with me tonight?'

'I . . . Yes, of course.'

He gave her the name and address of the restaurant. 'Would eight o'clock be too late for you? I have to visit my wife beforehand, hospitals being what they are.'

'Eight is fine.'

Over their apéritifs he said, 'I've considered your suggestion with the greatest care. The extraordinary thing is . . . I hesitate to imply that anything so fundamentally disgraceful could be Heaven-sent; but it's a fact that everything which happened last November, every circumstance connected with the drafting of that second will, might have been specifically arranged by Providence to fit in with what you proposed at my office.'

He went on to describe how one grey afternoon, the Mistral in grim possession of the valley, Abbott the know-all manservant absent, her father had suddenly changed his mind and had decided to make a new will after all. Nobody at La Bastide could witness it for two reasons: firstly because they were all minor beneficiaries, secondly because Edward Walden was determined not to have the matter discussed all over Montferrat, the Var, Southern France and beyond.

Rudd had drafted a will many months before, preceding a former change of mind; all he had to do now was to amend it where necessary, and this he did, arguing vehemently at the exclusion of Catherine and being flatly over-ruled. The two builders had been called in to witness it; neither knew any of the details, nor were they interested.

Her father's last words on the subject had been, 'Remember, David, I want this matter kept entirely private. I don't even want any of your colleagues in London to know. Not *one* word to anybody. If I hear so much as a whisper I'll know who to blame and I shall see that you pay for it.'

Catherine nodded, not trusting herself to speak, for still he had not committed himself; his next sentence could be preceded by a 'but' or a 'so'.

'So, in view of my wife's illness, and the tremendous bills I'm having to pay every week, sometimes every day, I've come to a decision. It terrifies me but I've come to it. I love Mary very much, I don't think I began to know how much until this dreadful complaint struck her down.' He stared despairingly into his glass as if trying to read his wife's future in it. 'I don't even know when or how she became such a part of me, I was never aware of it before, but there it is. When they cut her open, they cut me open. If she dies, I die.'

Catherine understood that like herself, but in a very different and more admirable way, he had nothing to lose. 'Then . . . you'll do it?'

'Yes.'

Relief flooded through her, carrying all manner of fears in its flow.

'However,' he said, 'there are a number of awkward circumstances . . .'

None, Catherine was sure, that she hadn't considered and reconsidered during the sleepless hours of last night.

'For instance, your mother . . .'

'But,' she said, cutting him short incisively, 'my mother's dead, Mr Rudd, isn't she?'

'Yes.' He nodded; then nodded again. 'Yes, of course, but that wasn't my point — the thing is, your mother came to an arrangement with Edward years ago. She agreed to relinquish all rights to his estate.'

'She never told me. But then . . . towards the end she became confused, irrational.'

He examined her intently, as if wondering what kind of a girl he was getting himself so perilously involved with. 'You don't quite grasp my point. Natalia Beaumont probably knows this—one imagines that your father didn't keep many secrets from her.'

'But if he never made a second will, if the first will you mentioned still stands, it doesn't matter whether she knows or not, does it? Whatever Mother may have agreed to, I'd be sole beneficiary.'

'Yes. Yes, of course.' He threw off his doubts and reached for the menu. They were in partnership.

'What are we going to *do*, David?'

Against the sparkling Mediterranean backdrop, its frivolity mocking the terrible situation in which their partnership had landed them, he shook his head grimly. 'Do? We have no option—short of buying a gun and shooting Abbott through the head. We do exactly what the bloody man wants.'

'Money, of course.'

'And a very great deal of it, make no mistake! I was always afraid of him, but I must say I thought it would be Natalia who caused the trouble.'

Catherine nodded, remembering her first conversation with Madame Beaumont among the roses, that sudden panic of doubt in which everything and everybody, even faithful Monsieur Gosselin, had seemed to be in league against her. 'She's gone away—visiting her brother in Belgium, I think they said.'

She now realized that in her anxiety she had not even noticed how strained and weary he looked. 'I'm sorry, I forgot to ask about your wife.'

'I was on the phone to London half the night. Complications—they're going to have to operate again.'

'But surely it's much too soon after . . . ?'

'Yes, yes—much too soon.' Clearly he couldn't bear to discuss it. 'Come on, let's get this over—see what Abbott's going to cost.'

But when Abbott opened the front door of La Bastide they found themselves confronted, not by the triumphantly self-satisfied villain they had expected, at once smugly deferential and jaunty at the thought of plunder to come, not even by the old Abbott with his air of knowing cynicism, but by a shrunken shadow of that man, pale blue eyes unable to look either of them in the face. Something disastrous to his interests had obviously happened in Catherine's brief absence from the house.

David Rudd, worrying about his wife perhaps, seemed less struck by the change than Catherine. He said, brusquely, 'All right, Abbott, let's get down to business, I've got to go back to London.'

The look which Abbott gave Catherine was almost one of appeal. 'No, sir. It isn't quite that way any more. What I mean is . . . I'm sure you'll appreciate that I had to tell Madame Beaumont—she seemed to know everything anyway.'

Catherine was appalled. 'Madame Beaumont? She's *here?*'

Abbott glanced fearfully towards the door of the salon, and lowered his voice. 'You must understand, Miss . . . Madam. I'm no longer in a position to . . . I have to protect my own interests.'

This remark was justified forthwith. The door of the salon opened and Nicholas Tate looked out. Beyond him, beyond the knowing eyes of Rembrandt's old woman, Catherine saw, sitting beside Natalia Beaumont on a sofa, her mother.

CHAPTER 7

Of all the inhabitants of La Bastide, and perhaps even of Montferrat, only Marianne Lavallier would have attached importance to the fact that Catherine had said, several times to several people, beginning with Madame Albert at the Hôtel de la Poste, that she had flown to Nice directly from New York; others might have forgotten this altogether, but as far as Marianne was concerned, in her romantic and earnest ignorance of travel and foreign places, one simply did not say that one had come from New York if one had in fact come from somewhere else, it didn't make sense. For her, New York was invested with particular interest; not only did its inhabitants live in towers of glass and steel, but it was the home of Liberty, a gift of France, and the birthplace of her lover, her son's father, of whom she had been fond in her own manner. However you looked at it, New York was definitely not London, birthplace no doubt of Wellington and Nelson, those enemies of France, a city which no Frenchwoman in her senses would desire to visit.

So, to Marianne as to no one else, the finding of Catherine's ticket among her underwear had revealed a remarkable anomaly: Mademoiselle had not flown from New York to Nice, as stated, but from New York to London, and then after a pause of five days, from London to Nice. She could even have been at Montferrat for her father's funeral if she had so wished. Disrespectful to the dead in Marianne's opinion.

Who else would have thought such a detail worth reporting to Madame Beaumont and Nicholas Tate?

At first these two, more sophisticated individuals, amused by further evidence of Madame Lavallier's snooping, had been inclined to ignore her immense discovery. Sophisticated minds very often ignore the suspicions of more simple souls, just as they tend to ignore the intuitions and omens, black cats, the pattern of tea-leaves, etcetera, to which simple souls attach so much importance. But then they had begun to ask their own, more sophisticated questions.

Why had Catherine never mentioned this visit to London, at any time to anybody? The very fact that she had gone out of her way to state and re-state that she had come directly from the United States seemed to imply, surely, that she didn't want anyone to know about those five days in London. Why? And what about her attitude to the whole matter of the will? An odd kind of certainty, even when they had told her that she was excluded from it altogether: a kind of defiance, yes.

So it was that even though Marianne's 'evidence' was nothing of the sort, Madame Beaumont had said, 'I think we'd be stupid to ignore it — we're not exactly overloaded with options.' And so it was that Nicholas had left for London immediately, and had immediately gone to see his friend, the ex-policeman who now ran his own private detective agency, asking him to answer two questions: had a certain Catherine Walden, a visitor from the USA, in London between the 9th and the 13th of the month, contacted a Mr David Rudd of the reputable firm of Mayer, Rudd and Wilson, and, if so, how often had they met? And had a certain Mrs Laura Walden, last heard of at a private nursing-home near Ascot, really died two years before, or was she by any chance still alive — not at the same nursing-home for sure but at another, more remote, even very remote, to which she could well have been moved between or just after those same dates.

So it was that the ex-policeman's minions had, in less than forty-eight hours, presented two answers: yes, Miss Walden and Mr Rudd had met at least five times between

the dates in question: at his office, at two out-of-the-way
restaurants, at her hotel: and yes, Mrs Laura Walden was
indeed alive and she had indeed been moved, not from
the nursing-home near Ascot, which had long since
ejected her due to her impossible behaviour, but from
another, near Bath, to an extremely remote establishment in Scotland.

And so it was that after a good deal of exhausting
argument and coercion, and a good deal of travel, Laura
Walden, Catherine's 'dead' mother, now sat in the salon
at La Bastide, with a glass of gin and tonic in one hand,
eyeing her daughter's shocked face with fuddled
amusement.

Catherine and David Rudd moved forward into the room
like sleepwalkers to find themselves confronted not only
by Mrs Walden, Natalia and Nicholas, but by Marianne
and Pascal Lavallier, Monsieur Gosselin and Jean-Michel
Beaumont, again in uniform. Seven pairs of eyes
regarded the two miscreants with varying mixtures of
anger, surprise, sorrow, shock and however slight,
however grudging -- admiration. Abbott, intent on
slipping away, was recalled peremptorily by Madame
Beaumont; followed Catherine and Mr Rudd into the big
room and closed the door behind him.

'Hello, dear!' said Mrs Walden. There was no way of
telling what she meant by the words: irony? malice? even
genuine welcome? The hand which steered the glass to
her inaccurately lipsticked mouth was unsteady. She was
in every way the wreck of a woman, sagging in a shapeless
dress (she, once the favourite clothes-horse of both Dior
and Balenciaga!) her belly distended by alcohol or
cirrhosis, no hint whatsoever of the beauty which had
been celebrated by every photographer and a dozen
fashionable portrait painters, merely blotched skin, puffy
over once fine bones, scanty white-blonde hair tucked

into a head scarf which she had fastened, also inaccurately, with a magnificent diamond brooch.

Natalia and Nicholas had been forced to reiterate and reiterate the vital nature of their mission in order to wean her away from doctors and nurses, though she herself, once she had stirred out of alcoholic inertia, seemed quite intrigued by the prospective journey and its bizarre purpose. It was her first foray into the outside world for six years, excepting the peregrinations from one nursing-home, where her tantrums made her no longer welcome, to the next where they would presently do so again.

Only because she had long ago severed relations with all her friends and family, never writing, not even letting them know where she was, had David Rudd considered Catherine's proposal in the first place. Word of her daughter's inheritance might or might not reach her at some point in the future, but she would show little interest (she had never been interested in anything but herself) and entertain no suspicions, why should she? The fact that she had renounced all claim upon her husband's estate didn't preclude his leaving everything to their only child, rather the reverse. In this context, Catherine's bland invention over an apéritif made possible sense: 'But my mother's dead, Mr Rudd, isn't she?' After due consideration he had thought it a reasonable risk to declare Laura Walden two years defunct, because as far as the world was concerned she had been defunct for many more years than that: dead but alas by no means properly buried.

It was one of Rudd's duties as old friend and lawyer to supervise Mrs Walden's housing, pay her bills, and generally make sure that she was satisfied with her self-imposed imprisonment, at least temporarily: the satisfaction was always short-lived. As he had explained to Catherine in the restaurant, this was another point at which Providence seemed to be in favour of their wrongdoing, for Edward Walden had always insisted that his wife's welfare was a purely private matter, not to be conducted in committee by Mayer, Rudd and Wilson but by David Rudd personally, using a private account. His reasons had been selfish, as ever; he didn't want Laura Walden's condition, and the part that he had played in causing it, to be discussed ad nauseam by old friends and enemies, even, God forbid, by the gossip-columnists who had always shown a rabid interest in their antics.

Yes indeed, it had all seemed a reasonable risk, but now . . . !

'I think,' said Natalia Beaumont, 'that we need hardly go into explanations. Abbott has told us that he's found one of the witnesses to Edward's second will. Where is the will, David?'

Ever since coming into the room Rudd had been considering the possibility of various denials, but his trained mind had dismissed them all as invalid. 'In my safe in London.'

'The sooner you put it in Monsieur Gosselin's hands the better.'

He nodded, almost absently, thinking of his wife and wondering how all those gigantic medical bills were going to be met, now that he himself would certainly be in prison.

'You might care,' said Lieutenant Beaumont, at his most pompous, 'to tell us the contents of the will here and now.'

'What you all expected. The entire estate divided into five equal parts—both mothers and sons, and Nicholas.'

'And a funny old lot too!' declared Laura Walden to nobody in particular. 'But then Edward was a funny old man.'

David Rudd, not unused to her, continued as if she hadn't spoken. 'Also various bequests, an extremely generous one as far as Abbott is concerned. But not,' he added, giving that traitor the look which he deserved, 'anything like as generous as the arrangement Miss Walden was prepared to make.'

'So easy,' said Nicholas Tate tartly, 'to be generous with other people's money!'

Catherine, who hadn't yet spoken, who hadn't even looked directly at any of them, was beginning to recover from the shock of her mother's presence. She noticed that Natalia was wearing pale pink, very soignée as usual; that Monsieur Gosselin's expression was one of kindly, if shocked, disapproval; that Marianne Lavallier was sitting very upright, her attractive face heavy with an outrage which betrayed how quickly she was about to lose her looks altogether, becoming just another lumpish peasant woman. Lieutenant Beaumont was again standing at attention, regarding her coldly as if already in command of the firing-squad. As for her mother, dear God what jangling memories of discord and unhappiness that ravaged, once-beautiful face aroused in her! Quarrels and tears in the small hours: bottles hidden at the back of bookshelves, under cushions; the long decline into stagnant torpor: the succession of 'nursing-homes': their last meeting in the visitors' room near Bath, and her fortunate desire to be removed from there at once: 'Impossible place, staffed by sadistic morons! And the *people!* Nobody, not a single soul of one's own class!' The prospect of a move to Scotland had delighted her.

Last of all, Catherine brought herself to glance at Pascal whose eye she had so far managed to avoid altogether. To her astonishment she found that he was smiling at her, no trace whatever of the animosity or censure displayed by the others. How utterly unalike they were, her two half-brothers! In comparison with Jean-Michel, Pascal looked untidy and raffish, but oh the warmth in that regard! She had never truly recognized it until now, or had recognized it and rejected it. This

generous smile, the assurance that she was not entirely
alone and outcast, enabled her to gather her wits, muster
some of her old courage, and say to Natalia Beaumont,
'All right, what are you going to do with us?'

Madame glanced down at her beringed fingers,
unwilling to meet that cold grey regard, by no means as
mortified as it ought to be, but time would amend that!
'We've discussed the matter at length, of course. I think
we have no choice . . .'

With typical, with thundering egotism, Mrs Walden
chose this moment to hold out her glass, tilting it to and
fro. 'Laura needs a little drinkie.'

Abbott, relieved to be doing something practical and
reassuring, attended to her needs. She gave her daughter
what could only be described as a roguish look and said,
'Telling everybody I was dead! Charming!'

Thus, typically, she evaded the reality of the situation,
since only one aspect was of any interest to her, the one
affecting Laura Walden. If she could not be leading
lady as, following her dramatic entrance, she doubtless
expected, then she would move the entire auditorium and
everyone in it, so that from her position at the back,
almost in the wings, she would appear to be stage-centre,
at least in her own estimation. She was quite unaware of
the fact that her demand for refreshment had interrupted
matters at a moment which was going to affect the entire
course of her daughter's life.

Natalia Beaumont continued: 'As far as you and David
are concerned we have no choice. Inspector Mattei is
waiting in the study.'

She had telephoned him immediately from Nice
airport. It had not been necessary to say more than, 'I
think that if you come immediately to La Bastide,
Inspector, I shall be able to honour my side of our . . .
understanding.'

At the sound of his name, Catherine's shred of courage

disappeared; it was so obviously a situation after his own Corsican heart.

'May as well go and get him now.' The Lieutenant was eager for action.

'You move,' said Pascal quietly, 'and I'll break your piddling little neck!' Before Jean-Michel could reply he turned on Madame Beaumont. '*We've* discussed it at length, *we* have no choice—who's we?'

'Naturally—your mother, Nicholas and I.'

'And,' said the dashing Lieutenant, 'I agree with them entirely, which puts you in a minority of one.'

Monsieur Gosselin cleared his throat and addressed the wall directly in front of him. 'I must say I think you're being extreme. I'm not defending Mademoiselle or my colleague, their action is indefensible, but surely . . .'

'This is a family matter, Monsieur.' Lieutenant Beaumont's grandfather would not have disapproved of his tone. 'Nothing to do with you. Inspector Mattei will decide what . . .'

'If you bring charges against Catherine,' said Pascal, wheeling back to Natalia Beaumont, 'I'll tell you what she's going to do—she's going to accuse your bone-headed son of attempted murder.'

There was a communal gasp. Marianne essayed a quavering 'Pascal!'

'And where will his glorious military career be then?'

In the silence which followed, Laura Walden said, 'You really are rather like Edward, aren't you? Better-looking—how furious he'd be to hear me say that!'

Catherine was shaking her head in bewilderment. Pascal enlightened her. 'Oh yes, it was that feeble-minded clot who attacked you on the terrace, and Inspector Mattei knows it.' He glared at Madame Beaumont, 'I bet you and he made some kind of cover-up deal—right?'

'Libel!' shouted his half-brother. 'I was with my unit

and I can prove it.'

'Libel my arse! Show us your right arm! I saw the dog grab you. Go on, show us your arm!'

Monsieur Gosselin was shaking his head in disbelief, not entirely willing to hide a gleam of satisfaction. 'Dear me, what an extremely foolish thing to do!' He caught David Rudd's eye and was not surprised to notice that he had seized upon this disclosure as the loophole which it assuredly was.

Catherine was looking at Jean-Michel in blank amazement. 'But . . . why? What were you trying to do?'

'I deny the . . . the whole ridiculous allegation.'

Pascal laughed. 'He was trying to scare you off and get me in trouble. He really is a little weak in the head.'

The Lieutenant moved forward, big hands twitching. 'You say one more word and I'll . . .'

'Jean, keep quiet!' The snap of his mother's voice silenced him. Of course this was the exact eventuality she had feared on first hearing of his preposterous exploit; the situation which that stupidity had now engendered was only a little less deplorable than the necessity of coming to an 'understanding' with Inspector Mattei. Her quick mind accepted the fact that the 'understanding' no longer existed and that her son's career was still in jeopardy. A large sum of money, which she would soon be able to afford, would settle Mattei, but Pascal was another matter. She managed a charming smile. 'You won't encourage Mademoiselle to bring any such charges. Your place is with *us*, we all belong to the same family, we share the same interests.'

'Fuck the family! It's a farce, it doesn't even exist, and the only interest you all share is Edward Walden's money.'

Edward Walden's widow found this straight-talking extremely funny. She laughed immoderately, gin slopping down the front of her dress, while Marianne tried, without conviction, to silence her son. 'Madame Beaumont's right. It's a family matter, and the least you can do is . . .'

'Bullshit! What's the matter with you, Mother? Have you forgotten that they tried to pin that assault on *me*? You're all a bunch of money-mad hypocrites!'

'That's right, boy,' cried Laura Walden, always one to side with the best-looking man in the room. 'You give it to them! Oh, this is most entertaining!' She attempted to put her glass on a nearby table but missed it by several inches. Abbott darted forward, edging between the combatants, to clear up the mess; the carpet was an Aubusson.

Meanwhile Pascal had turned to Catherine, placing himself squarely between her and David Rudd. 'You don't have to let them get away with this. You're still his daughter, you're entitled to a share of the money.' He saw the doubt in her face, and added, 'Don't you see? They daren't accuse *you* of a thing, or bang go the Dummy's prospects! Fight them!'

As if he had charged her with his own furious elation she felt the adrenelin flare through her; he made all things seem possible. 'Maybe I will at that!'

'No,' said Natalia Beaumont, 'I don't think so.' She looked at Laura Walden who was still mopping the front of her dress with a cloth supplied by Abbott. 'Why do you think Nicholas and I went to so much trouble to find your mother and bring her here?'

Though this question had naturally flashed through Catherine's mind as soon as she saw that intransigent parent, it had been lost among a welter of more pressing problems.

'For some reason we'd never really talked about it before, but when we did we realized that Edward had dropped quite a number of . . . of hints over the years.'

'We weren't sure, and so—' Nicholas gestured—'it would only have been your word against ours. What we needed was proof.'

'And proof,' added Natalia complacently, 'is what we now have. Laura?'

'Yes, dear.'

'Tell her.'

'Tell who what?' She looked up from rearranging her neckline, and gazed around at them as if she had momentarily forgotten who they all were and what she was doing in their company.

'Tell Catherine,' said Madame Beaumont patiently, 'why Edward cut her out of his will.'

'Oh that!' The bleary eyes found her daughter's face among the others. 'Very simple, dear, I'm afraid you're not his child.'

All the blood drained out of the girl's cheeks. Pascal, thinking that she was about to faint, took a firm grip of her arm. It seemed to Catherine that she had emitted some kind of cry, loud, even deafening, in the dead silence which greeted this disclosure. The floor was billowing under her feet and the room had receded; she was unable to bring it back into proper focus. Knowing her mother as she did, it never for a moment entered her reeling mind to doubt what she had just heard. All the rancorous things which that selfish woman had been saying to her all her life were gathered together in this paralysing revelation.

David Rudd said, 'Jesus Christ!' The others were gaping at her with varying expressions of shock or complacency.

'That,' continued Laura Walden, seemingly unaware of the devastation she had just unleashed, 'is why he got so cross and threw me out. Though what *he* had to be cross about, God alone knows—carrying on with that dreadful young Frenchman and getting himself sacked from the Diplomatic! Naturally I went straight out and found myself a nice man. I wasn't exactly *plain*.'

'What . . . what man, Mother?'

'Charlie Ackroyd, dear, you're like him too—oh, he *was* handsome! I'd have told you áll about it if he hadn't gone and got himself killed in that Bentley. After a Hunt Ball, needless to say! I really have had the most appalling luck with men.'

'So you see—' only Natalia Beaumont's eyes betrayed her satisfaction—'you're not exactly in a position to contest the will, are you? It has nothing to do with you and never had.'

More gently, touched by her stricken face, Nicholas said, 'You hadn't been born when he made it, and at the time your mother hadn't yet left him. He was still hoping . . .' He glanced at Mrs Walden, embarrassed.

But there was no need to feel embarrassment on that lady's account. 'Oh yes,' she said, a trifle indistinctly because her mouth was inside her glass, 'he wanted to have several sons.' She giggled. 'Well, he did, but not by me.'

David Rudd sighed and shook his head. 'So Edward gets the last laugh, as usual. Abbott, I need a drink. Catherine, I'm so sorry . . .'

She shook her head, still staggering from that knockout blow. Her whole being was now invaded by a creeping sense of shame, a recognition of her own infinite stupidity. She had dared to defy a Providence which had been against her all her life; of course she could never have won. What pride! What a fall! And how the old clichés always come to make sense in the end: she wished fervently that a divine hand would roll the Aubusson aside and open the floor, removing her from all these people, witnesses to her humiliation. She wanted to be back, alone, in her wretched little New York apartment.

Paul Gosselin, on the other hand, fully understood the relief, the release from tension, which had permitted his fellow-lawyer to call for a drink. He also understood that David Rudd was waiting for him to define the position:

with particular regard to a certain merciful contingency. 'The situation is now clear. Edward Walden's second will exists and is legal, and Mademoiselle Catherine is excluded from it for a very obvious reason. She and Monsieur Rudd made a mistake . . .' He held up a hand to silence the foreseen chorus of invective. 'Yes, a *criminal* mistake for which, in the normal course of events, they would be brought to judgement and would pay dearly. However, if you expose them you will be doing so at the expense of Lieutenant Beaumont's military career. Make no mistake — a charge of attempted murder, proven or not, will certainly lose him his commission. Therefore you have no alternative but to let them go free.' No judge could have summed up the matter more clearly or concisely. The greenish eyes met Catherine's for a second, shyly, (What an extraordinary young woman!) and then took refuge elsewhere. She said, 'Thank you, Monsieur Gosselin, for all your kindness.'

He turned and looked at the Beaumonts, mother and son, at Nicholas Tate, at Marianne Lavallier. 'You agree?'

There was a pause. Then, one by one, they nodded their assent. Madame Beaumont no doubt spoke for all of them when she added, 'I agree only because I must.'

It was all too much for the dashing Lieutenant, who burst out with, 'But, Mother, I wasn't going to *murder* her, that's absolute nonsense, I only . . .'

'Jean, for heaven's sake, why are you such a . . . ?' Motherly discretion caught her by the heels, but only just, and forced her to end, 'Use your brain, dear, please.'

Jean-Michel subsided, still mutinous. Understanding would perhaps filter through eventually.

'In that case,' said Monsieur Gosselin, already moving with the speed which is always so surprising in large men, 'I shall tell Mattei that there's been a mistake, his services are not required after all.' Abbott jumped to open the door for him, and before any of them could think of a logical reason for detaining him he was gone.

Madame Beaumont stood up and confronted Catherine and David Rudd. 'I hope you both realize how extremely lucky you are. Only my son's . . . hot-headedness permits you to leave this house without being under arrest. David, you and I have certain arrangements to make.' And, glancing at Catherine: 'Isabelle has already packed your things. I suggest you leave at once.'

Catherine looked beyond her at the people who had, until a few minutes ago, played so important a part in her life. They seemed to be frozen into immobility, like puppets abandoned by their master. She turned and, pursued by the demons of shame and inadequacy and her own presumption, fled from the room.

She fled across the hall, not even glancing at Rembrandt's old woman whose wise eyes would only be saying, 'Stupid little girl! I knew it all the time.' She wasn't aware of Abbott following her with her suitcase, not even aware of Pascal who was calling out, 'Catherine, wait! I have to speak to you.' All she wanted was to be away from this place which she had started by hating and ended by hating, with a brief and brainless period of infatuation between.

She fell into her car, started it, accelerated away with an erratic abandon which put even Marianne Lavallier to shame. Pascal, running beside her, saw only a tight, bloodless and stricken face. He cried out to Abbott, who had just managed to thrust the suitcase into the back seat, 'My God, she shouldn't be driving, she doesn't know what she's doing!' The dust of Catherine's violent departure was enshrouding them both.

CHAPTER 8

She would not, in the future, remember anything about that perilous drive down the mountain road. After a time she did indeed become aware of a car behind her; and then of the fact that its driver was sounding his horn furiously. Well, if somebody wanted to overtake let them do so! She didn't realize that her own breakneck speed and the corkscrew corners made this impossible.

Pascal was in despair, as terrified by the risks she was taking as Catherine ought to have been but was not. If he couldn't pass and bring her gradually to some kind of standstill, there was no doubt in his mind that she, like many another before her, was going to end up in a tangle of blazing wreckage a couple of hundred feet below.

Only when she had taken a notorious bend much too fast and had actually cannoned into one of the crooked stone bollards which were all that separated her from death, did rational thought cause her to brake; and while she was braking Pascal took his own life in his hands, for there was a blind corner dead ahead, and roared past her, tyres screeching.

Even then she didn't recognize him; couldn't understand why this idiot was now slowing down, blocking the road, and finally coming to such an awkward standstill that she too was forced to stop.

Pascal jumped out of his Mercedes and advanced upon her in the fury of overwhelming relief. When she realized who it was she gave a great gasp, like a drowning person fighting for air, buried her face in her hands, and let her head fall forward on to the steering-wheel. His ensuing diatribe, a release of terror, passed right over her head, literally.

She came to her sense to find herself leaning against a rock not far from the road; their two cars were neatly parked nearby. Pascal was standing in front of her, wild-eyed and panting, his sweaty shirt clinging to his body. Seeing his face, she remembered the kindness which had given her courage in another place, in another life, in an appalling room stuffed with valuable treasures. It seemed long ago.

He took her by the shoulders and pushed her into a sitting position against the rock. She closed her eyes and leaned back, exhausted, letting the hot sun enfold her. A measureless amount of time then passed, perhaps a minute, perhaps an hour, she would never know. When she opened her eyes again, he was sitting quietly beside her, holding a bottle of wine. He thrust it at her and said, 'Drink! Go on, it doesn't matter whether you like it or not.'

She obeyed, spluttering; she had never been able to master the trick of drinking out of a bottle. After this they again sat in silence. Then she said, 'Do you always carry bottles of wine around with you?'

'Always. They come in handy.' He wiped the neck and handed it to her again. This time she was aware of its roughness, which shocked her: all to the good. When it was his turn he drank thirstily, and then smiled. Watching him, she found that she too was smiling — and so short a time ago she had imagined that she would never smile again. 'I suppose we're both thinking the same thing.'

'Of course. We always do.'

'Lapalisse. That lousy champagne.'

He nodded. 'We may not be related but we're still awfully alike — except you're probably worse than I am. What a thing to do, what a game! And you nearly brought it off!'

She caught her breath, face puckering. He thought,

mistakenly, that she was going to burst into tears.
Instead: 'Oh God, I feel such a *fool*, Pascal!'

'One does. We'd better drink to that stupid oaf, Jean-
Michel — he saved your bacon.'

They drank. After a moment's thought he smiled
again. Catherine said, 'And I know exactly what you're
thinking now.'

'What?'

'You're thinking that at Lapalisse *you* imagined I was
your half-sister, and *I* imagined you were after my
money.'

'Right.'

'No half-sister, no money!'

Still smiling, they regarded each other with a kind of
frank intimacy which circumstance had always denied to
them before. He said, 'Know when my game ended, as far
as you were concerned?'

She shook her head.

'When those pompous pricks came up that afternoon
and told you he'd cut you right out of his will. You were
great, you never put a foot wrong, you didn't give them so
much as half a millimetre, and I thought, "By God, that
girl's too good to miss, get her!" '

'So?'

'So, Mademoiselle, when you're feeling better, and if
you're agreeable, why don't we drive down there and find
a nice little hotel with a nice big bed? We'll register as
Monsieur and Madame . . . What do you fancy?'

'*Lieutenant* and Madame Jean-Michel Beaumont.'

'Of course! And we'll send him the bill.' Laughing, he
put an arm around her and leaned closer to whisper in
her ear. 'If you're a good girl I might even marry you, and
then . . .'

'Big deal!'

'No, let me finish, it's a good joke. Then, with Mother's
share, we'd control nearly half that money anyway—can

you see their faces?'

So they sat there in the sun, laughing like children, sharing their bottle of wine, the glittering world spread out at their feet.